# THE PITCHFORK MURDER

KAREN YOCHIM

ISBN: 1500284653

ISBN 13: 9781500284657

Library of Congress Control Number: 2014913557
CreateSpace Independent Publishing Platform
North Charleston, South Carolina

Dedicated to: Chandler Steffens


*We have never forgotten.*

*We still seek answers.*

*For there is nothing hidden that will not be disclosed, and nothing concealed that will not be known or brought out into the open.* Luke 8:17 NIV

Many thanks to Jeff Davis Taylor, Anne Ruth, Delia Taylor, Roland Rivette, St. Landry Sheriff's Office, Lt. Allen Venable of the Metro Crime Unit, Lafayette Parish Sheriff's Office; Becky McKay, Orlando Fire Department Communications Supervisor, Retired; Arnaudville Police Department, Tony Groves, Paul Marx KBON; Murray Conque, Dan Liddy, Barry Innes, Rob McDaniel, Twinkle Yochim, Barry Fouts, Candy Palumbo, Jimmy T. Simmons, Lauren Johnson, Jerry Domingeaux, Teresa Esther Chapoy, Tony LeClerc, and Anonymous, (you know who you are.)

# 1

# ADMINISTRATIVE LEAVE

It was a 911 call that kicked it all off. I responded to the call first because I was the closest to the caller's address at that moment, and quickly drove the half-mile to help her. The house is at the end of a dirt road almost to the town limits with acres of soybean fields rolling in back of it to a distant tree line. It has a corrugated metal roof and board and batten siding and is partially shaded by a huge magnolia tree.

Two buzzards were pecking at a deer hide someone had tossed to the drainage ditch at the side of the road, and a few black and white spotted hens were scratching for grubs and worms in the front yard, as a gleaming white rooster stood guard over them. A shiny green double cab pickup was parked in the shell driveway, a gleaming metal toolbox bolted to the truck bed.

I parked in back of the pickup and walked toward the porch listening hard for any sounds coming from the house. The woman who called in claimed her husband was drunk and raving and scaring her, but the scene was quiet and still except for a mockingbird pretending to be a cardinal, and the drowsy hum of cicadas. A light breeze drifted through causing a tinny sound from wind chimes at the far end of the porch. A few green hummingbirds whirred their wings at a feeder hanging from a hook.

An orange cat curled on a freshly painted red metal glider with bright yellow cushions paid no mind to me as I knocked on the front door. It was open a few inches and I nudged it open a foot further. I could see into a dim living room, and beyond to the entryway of a large well-lighted country kitchen.

` A woman was lying motionless on the floor of the kitchen, so I hurried over the threshold and on through the living room to reach her side. Blood had spread over her blouse and her eyes stared at the ceiling. One arm had flopped across her torso and the other was flung out on the tile floor. I hunkered down and pulled my pistol, looking around the room, just as a wild eyed man with red sweating face juggled a handgun as he came hurtling out from a door at the far end of the kitchen, headed for the back door. In a second, he had both yanked open the back door and taken a pot shot in my direction, the bullet going straight through the living room and shattering a glass pane of the front door.

I shot him in the head just one second before he stepped foot outside the doorway. He fell onto the back cement steps just as Chief Ira pulled up outside into the front yard. Within ten minutes, that house was a mob scene. The flowerbed outside was flattened and stomped over as EMTs, police, and crime scene techs stormed onto the scene. Television crews from Lafayette and Eustis swarmed around outside.

Beyond the swarm of responders, out on the dirt road, neighbors from a mile in each direction rapidly gathered to stand and stare. One of them, the victim's cousin, broke away from the lineup to lead a howling hound from a kennel in the back yard away to her own home. It was a solemn circus that went on for hours until way past dark. The only thing missing was a hot dog vendor and someone hawking beer and soft drinks.

And that is how I was put on administrative leave with pay until this shooting could be assessed first by Sheriff Quebedeaux's St. Beatrice Parish Investigative Division, and then Internal Affairs. There was no telling how long the investigation would take as it can sometimes go on for many months, even years.

Along with all the rest of the turmoil this kicked up, Gus Vidrine, the dead man's brother let it be known around town that it would be in my best interest to watch my back. As it turned out it was in Gus' best interest to watch *his* back because before his brother and sister-in-law were even buried, one of the local rooster fights he regularly attended was busted and close to seventy-five gamblers and participants were arrested in one swift takedown by Sheriff Quebedeaux's deputies. They were all hauled off to jail in a bus: the same confiscated bus that picked the gamblers up at the Lagniappe Bar parking lot to drive them to Horace Duchamp's metal building in the woods back of his barn where the fights were held.

St. Beatrice is usually quiet, but that particular month was chaotic. A local crackhead, Skinny Dupuis, was under suspicion because he was arrested for possession and yet was released within twenty-four hours. Rightly or wrongly, Skinny was quickly targeted as the one who ratted out the fight arena. Skinny washed up onto a rise of sediment that had silted up under one of the town's small cement bridges a few days after the bust. By that time, the body was soggy and bloated, his customary suntan faded away, and the skin bluish and pale as the belly of a catfish.

In case you're wondering how anyone could get himself murdered over a rooster fight, you may not know just how big the stakes are and the kind of money that flies around at those events. Back when I was young, dumb, and full of it, my cousin Stubs and I used to drive some weekends over to the towns of Cankton or Sunset for the fights. These were the major hot spots in all of Louisiana for this before the Louisiana legislature voted, (a close vote), to make rooster fights illegal in 2008, the last state to do so.

The ten thousand square foot Sunset arena is the largest, with a capacity of over six hundred people, although the building in Cankton is also huge. Rooster fights were always totally integrated with young, old, blacks, whites, Hispanics, and even small children attending. While males were in the majority, wives and girl friends often attended as well, although most of the men preferred to keep to themselves just how much money they won…or lost.

There was a time in Louisiana when gamblers from all over the world came to Sunset with suitcases full of cash for rooster fights. The biggest bet I ever witnessed was for fifty thousand dollars, however a friend of mine, a handler, who was involved in these events for many years witnessed an eighty thousand dollar bet go down.

Ironically, three of the men arrested at Horace's arena were from Miami and drove up to Louisiana a few times a year for the rooster fights in Slidell. This was the first time they'd ever decided to drive on over to Cajun country to gamble on the fights. They were furious, bailed out of the Parish jail over in Eustis immediately, paid a local to drive them to the Lagniappe Bar parking lot, and after throwing down a few fast boilermakers in the bar and a lot of complaining about their situation to Roy, the bartender, they roared off in their gleaming black Caddy back to Florida.

I had my own ideas about what might have happened to Skinny and who might have done him in, but because of the suspension wasn't allowed to help with the investigation, so kept my thoughts to myself. Everything depends on how you look at it, so instead of feeling awkward and impatient with the ongoing investigation, I distracted myself at home working on a tool shed, a small cypress structure with metal roof that I was patching and tightening up. The tool shed stood twenty feet from another building that sheltered a '66 Mustang I was restoring, bit by bit, as much as time and money allowed. If the investigation dragged on long enough, I hoped to get more work done on the Mustang as well.

My wife, Georgette, had to quit her job at a travel agency in Lafayette because of a persistent series of migraines that had become more and more debilitating during the past year. She was fine on the job until the onset of a migraine, and as the headaches became more and more severe, she had to take meds and lie down in a dark bedroom for sometimes as long as a day and a night. We didn't know if she'd ever be able to hold a job in future.

Our house sits on ten acres a few miles out of town, and there was always plenty of work to do around the place, and work was all I knew to do to get through the backlash of shooting a man. I had never had to shoot anyone in all the ten years I'd been with the Department. There were only two times I'd had to even fire my pistol while on duty.

One time was to shoot a copperhead coiled with fangs out in the middle of the town park with kids playing nearby; and the other time was the morning a hungry coyote carried off a woman's Pomeranian while she was visiting a grave in the St. Beatrice cemetery in back of St. Joe's. I didn't lose any sleep over shooting Leon Vidrine, but I did have a hard time getting it out of my mind, so I worked extra hard finding the heavier the work I did, the less the murder scene replayed in my head. I would exhaust myself so that by late afternoon all I thought about was a few beers and kicking back with Georgette.

One night almost a month after the shooting, she fixed a shrimp stew and baked one of her pecan cream-filled cakes. As we sat at the kitchen table, I laughed and asked her why she was buttering me up.

"Actually," and she gave me a little smile, "I am guilty of doing just that." She tapped the napkin to her mouth, pausing to smooth it back onto her lap. "A friend from way back in high school wrote me a long letter. Mallory Jenks is her name. You may have seen her Christmas cards that come each year. She always tries to get me to go back to our hometown and attend one of the class reunions. And as you well know I have never had any interest in ever going back to Florida." Georgette took a sip of coffee avoiding my eyes.

"I remember the name."

"Well, this time she is really coming after me about it. She practically begged me to go down there for this year's reunion. She says it's going to be great. One of our classmates is a big star in Nashville, and Bucky is going to bring his band along and play for the Saturday night dance. It's going to be a big deal. They will even be shooting the performance for his next music video."

"So who's this guy again?"

"Bucky Holmes. You've heard his songs. *Meet Me Halfway, Full House Beats a Pair, Overdrive.*"

"Sure. I know those songs. You know that guy? How come you never said anything?"

She frowned. "Didn't I? I must have mentioned it at least once. Maybe not."

"So I'm guessing you want to fly down to the reunion? Sure. Why not? Sounds like you'll have a good time with your old friends. You haven't seen any of them for over twenty years, right?"

"Oh, no," she said in alarm "That's not what I had in mind at all. I would never go without you. I just couldn't. You know I've stayed away on purpose all these years. I'm only going cause Mallory is making such a fuss about it."

"Me? But, no, I can't leave right now. I'm finally getting the time to work on the shed and the Mustang."

She paused and looked at her plate where there was still a small piece of cake. "I was hoping you'd drive us down there. We could catch a break from all that's happened around here and have ourselves a mini vacation. We could drive down, take turns at the wheel, and be there in twelve hours...then it's only a weekend at the new Gulf front hotel where many will be staying. We could be there for the Friday night party, and the Saturday luncheon and then the big dance when Bucky and his band will be playing. We could be out of there Sunday soon as we have breakfast, and be back here late that night."

"Sounds like you really want to go," I said, stalling for time while I tried to think how to get out of this.

"I really want to go with you. Not alone though." Her blue eyes were bright and almost pleading. I had a sinking feeling that I was getting sucked into an area where I had absolutely no interest. I had never even gone to one of my own class reunions, and

I sure wasn't interested in going to someone else's, even if it was Georgette's. My dessert plate was empty by then, and I set the fork down on it and lined the napkin up next to it, playing for time.

"Let me think about it for a little while," I said. "I still think it'd be a whole lot easier for me to drive you to the airport in Lafayette. You would be there in about an hour and a half. Beats the hell out of driving all day. That's a long haul for one weekend. And don't forget, then we have to drive all the way back."

She shook her head. "If you won't go, I don't go. I'm not going alone."

"But, your friend Mallory would probably be glad to pick you up at the airport and take you home with her or you can stay at the hotel. Catch up with your friends. I don't know any of those people."

"The shed and the Mustang will be there when we get back, so what's the big hurry all of a sudden? You really need to catch a break. You shot a man who needed to get shot, but I know it's taken a lot out of you. I'd really like to see you get away for a while. You think you're past this, but a wife can tell more than you think, and you're not over this yet. And nobody would expect you to be either."

She stood and started picking up the plates, stopping to kiss my forehead as she passed on the way to the sink. "Think about it and get back with me, will you? It would mean a lot. And it's good timing cause once the Chief calls you back to duty, you won't get such a good chance to get away for a long while."

I went into the den and took out a new poker deck from the drawer of the coffee table and started shuffling the stiff cards to help me think it over. I shuffled and reshuffled, fanned them out, picked them up, cut them, shuffled again, reshuffled. This went on for a good ten minutes until Georgette came into the den to join me.

"Want to play a hand or two?" she asked.

I shuffled once more, smacked the deck down on the coffee table, and waited. Georgette cut the deck her usual way, by just lifting a few cards from the top. Only this time she turned them over to show the bottom card.

"Ha!" she said. "The two of hearts. Looks like you decided to go with me after all." She leaned over and kissed me on the mouth to seal the deal. "Thank you, Edmond Dantés," she said. (My full name is Edmond Dantés Mallet, but she often calls me Edmond Dantés because she likes the name.) She gave me such a loving look, I didn't bother to remind her that I hadn't decided anything yet.

Then, what the hell, I accepted my fate, smacked the deck back into place and dealt us five cards each, turning over the last card dealt, announced that spades were trump, and we proceeded to play half a dozen hands of *bourrée* at our usual ante of two bucks a game. I won as usual, but that didn't help me to like the idea of hauling us off to Florida in a few days, but I'm smart enough to know when I've been had, and also smart enough to keep my mouth shut about it. The fix was in.

# 2

# THE BIJOU ROYALE

If you've ever made the trip on I-10 from Louisiana to Florida, then you know once you've crossed the twenty minute long Atchafalaya Swamp bridge, and gone over the famous riveted bridge over the Mississippi River at Baton Rouge, you've only got roughly a half hour to the Mississippi State line.

Soon as we crossed it and passed a desolate stretch of scrub and pines, Georgette stared out her window and said, "There's where that horrible Lynyrd Skynyrd plane crash happened. Upsets me just to pass by here." She shuddered and shook her head. "Hurts me just to think about it."

"No, that was up near McComb in Gillsburg," I corrected her.

"Are you sure?"

"I'm sure. I've seen the exact place right where the plane went down."

"One of my friends told me this was the place when we passed through here going to Talladega for

Nascar one year," she said, picking up the thermos to pour us more coffee.

"Well, your friend was wrong."

"I can always count on you to keep me honest. Must be why I married you. Here, have some coffee." She held a cup steady near my arm until I could take it from her.

In a little over an hour we had crossed Mississippi, and then passed quickly through Alabama to the tunnel at Mobile and once through that were on the long sweeping bridge across Mobile Bay with the huge U.S. Alabama looming large to the right while we cruised over the glittering coffee-colored waters of the bay.

From there, it's just minutes before you cross the Florida State line, and then you are headed for a long, boring five-hour stretch of flatland and piney woods, so you better keep the coffee thermos filled or you'll wind up asleep at the wheel. Whenever Georgette and I travel, we take a thermos full of strongly brewed coffee. She always packs sandwiches and snack food so we only have to stop when it's time to gas up. This saves us travel time, and it was a good thing we were so practiced at this, because the drive through the Panhandle feels as long as the drive through Texas, even though crossing Texas takes us two days and not just five hours.

When we drive anywhere, we generally keep a Classic Rock station on the radio and it's our habit for me to announce what each song is as soon as I've identified it by the opening chords. Sometimes I can tell as soon as the first chord what the song is, and Georgette likes this. She always shakes her head and says how she wishes she could do that as often as I do. She has never beaten me at this game, but she came close a few times. So we ran through a lot of songs before she had to find another station because we had driven out of the range of the one in Mobile.

About halfway across when we were close to Marianna, it was time to stop for gas, and I weakened and let Georgette take over the driving for a while. She drove until we got well past Tallahassee while I leaned my head back and closed my eyes, and then I took over again because I prefer to do the driving. It's not that I don't know there are good women drivers out there, but Georgette isn't one of them and I get tired of trying not to criticize.

So I drove the rest of the way to Bonita City, which lies on the Gulf Coast not too far south of Clearwater. As we passed condo after condo, and ran into more and more traffic, Georgette moaned. "What has happened to Bonita City? It was nothing like this when I left. It used to be a quiet secluded, laid back Gulf Coast town. Now look at it. I can't believe how crowded it is. I almost wish we stayed home."

That was encouraging. "It's not too late to turn around. We could stay overnight in Tallahassee after we eat dinner in a really good restaurant."

She looked over at me and laughed. "You'd like that wouldn't you? Nice try, Edmond Dantés." She returned her gaze to the long row of condos blocking the view of the water. "This was all one long stretch of Australian pine trees when I was in high school. God! Cement high rises everywhere you look."

"What's the name of that hotel again?"

"Bijou Royale."

"How original. Sounds like something out of James Bond. I think that's it up ahead." The high-rise hotel did not look at all like a jewel or even a royal jewel. With its cement block construction, it looked more like a hospital. I slowed, signaled and turned off into a tightly packed parking lot, then drove to what looked like an Emergency Room entrance under a cement overhang and parked. I went around to the trunk of the Civic for our two suitcases, then handed off the keys to the valet and the suitcases to the bellman as the valet opened the door for Georgette.

She blinked as she stepped out of the car look-ing somewhat dazed from the long drive as she smoothed her blouse and skirt. I reached out to take her hand, and we walked on into the well-lighted lobby and marched on up to a short line at the re-ception desk. There were cushy upholstered chairs and pastel couches scattered around the expansive lobby. A few people sat here and there reading news-papers, as soft music played through the intercom.

Georgette nudged me with an elbow and nodded to a tall balding man a few steps ahead of us. "He was the first date I ever had in my life. He brought me a corsage. First corsage I ever had too. Come to think of it, maybe the only one I ever had," she whispered, her hand half covering her mouth.

I took a deep breath. And so it began. I was not looking forward to meeting and making small talk with a whole bunch of people I didn't know. I was tired from the trip, and wanted nothing but a few beers, a hot dinner, and flopping on the hotel bed for a good movie, maybe two good movies. I didn't want to spoil her weekend by letting on I was already bored, but I knew it was not going to be easy to keep it hidden either.

Fortunately, the man ahead of us didn't notice Georgette when he turned away from registering and headed off to the elevators, so I was spared a conversation with him before we even got up to the room. And by the time we did get to our room on the twelfth floor, I was pleasantly surprised. There was a king-sized bed, a couch, some easy chairs, a fancy cabinet for the television set, and a great view of the smooth Gulf from the ten-foot wide windows. I tipped the bellman and Georgette took my hand and pulled me toward the view.

"Look down there. There's a Tiki bar at the edge of the pool. You can go down and have a drink while I hang up our clothes. Good idea?"

"I was going to take a hot shower first, but you talked me into it." I rubbed my hands together in anticipation. The sun was still bright but it was beginning its descent and I knew we didn't have much afternoon left. "You coming down? Want to get in that pool?"

"I don't know. I doubt it. Looks too crowded for comfort."

She went up on tiptoe and gave me a hug. "Thank you, sweetheart, for bringing me. I know you'd rather be working on your Mustang, but this could be fun. Tonight's the cocktail party. You can take a shower after you unwind a little down there at the bar."

I started toward the door. "And if you run into somebody with long jet black straight hair and really built down there at poolside, ask if her name is Mallory. She'll probably be wearing a thong bikini if I know Mallory. Watch out though for her husband, C.J. He's a brute. I think he was even a professional wrestler at one time. Mallory knows everything about everybody we went to school with, by the way. She's got a fantastic memory for details, especially details people would rather forget."

"I'll leave all the socializing up to you. I'm headed straight for a cold one."

As I left our room, Georgette had already begun shaking out a black dress to hang in the sliding door closet.

I blinked in the bright sunlight as I stepped out of the back entrance to the pool and made my way past a long row of lounges where about thirty people talked and laughed as they reunited with old friends. Some of the people in the water hung on to the edge of the pool, side by side, as they visited with one another and scissor-kicked their legs in back of them for exercise.

At the palm-thatched pool bar, there were a dozen cushioned rattan bar stools mostly in use with a few men standing around as they held their drinks and talked with friends. I found one stool over to the side nearest the Gulf and found myself seated next to a man about my age with a buzz cut who nodded to me as I caught the barkeep's eye and pointed to the Bud my new neighbor was drinking.

"You part of the group?" he asked.

"My wife is."

"My name's Rick Wagner." He held out his hand. "What's your wife's name? I must know her."

"Georgette."

"Georgette, Georgette." He clicked his fingers, then smiled. "Georgette Rhodes. Right?"

The barman brought my Bud and I gave him our room number. I picked up the bottle and lightly tapped it against his. "Here's to you, Rick," I said.

"Likewise," he said, and we spun on our stools to watch the swimmers. "Would you look at that," he said, and nodded toward a woman who was entering the pool area from the hotel. She wore dark glasses, a bright colored sarong and a black straw wide brimmed hat and high-heeled sandals. As soon as she found an empty chaise, she removed the sarong. Underneath it she wore a tiny sliver of a black bikini and as soon as she stretched out on the chaise, she leaned her head back and tilted the straw hat over her face, making it clear that she was distancing herself from the reunion crowd in order to take a nap.

"So who is she?"

"She is none other than our very own Daphne. A woman with a very strange past. It's a long story."

"So tell me."

"She was one of our cheerleaders, and involved with a football player….a star football player…who was murdered in our senior year. It was a gruesome murder and it was written up in all the national tabloids. They called it the Pitchfork Murder, because somebody skewered him through the chest and neck with a pitchfork and stuck him up on the door of a stall in his parents' barn."

Rick had my attention. "And they never found who did it?"

"They interrogated everybody and anybody for months, years even. The Sheriff's office went on high alert and stayed on high alert. The whole town was hysterical. The guy, Myron Miller, had a full scholarship to Tallahassee playing for the Seminoles, and was headed there for summer training soon as school let out. Everybody liked him, and everybody was in shock."

"So what about her?" I gestured with my beer toward Daphne.

"Get this. She was his girl friend, and they were both voted to be Prom King and Queen which was only a few weeks away. They dragged her in for interrogation over and over and over. And they kept doing it for months after that. Going over and over her story, hoping to find some little detail she may have remembered that would lead them to solving the case. Finally she got exhausted with all of it, went away to nursing school somewhere around Houston, and never came back to town far as I know. I haven't seen her for a long time. Surprised she even came back for this."

A man in slacks and a polo shirt crossed over to Daphne's side and sat on the edge of her chaise. She slightly lifted the brim of her hat to talk with him for a minute, and then he got up and walked away as she placed the hat back flat over her face.

"She got rid of him quick," Rick laughed. He made a circling motion with his forefinger to the bartender for more beers.

"So how come a barn? Was Myron a farmer?"

"His father was. That was back when there were still some farms left out east of here. Once the developers swarmed in and started tearing everything down and packing in wall-to-wall houses for the Yankee invasion, those farms bit the dust."

"So the barn's gone now?"

"Not sure. I've been living in Macon for a long while. I could find out pretty quick though if you really want to know."

"Cold-case stories always interest me."

"You a cop or something?"

"Or something. I'm on administrative leave right now."

He held up his hands. "Don't tell me. You had to shoot somebody."

I just looked at him without answering.

Rick's eyes widened. "No shit? Guy must have asked for it, huh?"

"You could say that. He had just shot his wife and was trying for me."

Rick slowly shook his head. "No shortage of assholes in this world. Right? They don't pay you guys enough to get shot at."

We drank in silence for a while, and watched the scene at the pool. Then Georgette came out of the hotel door and shading her eyes with her hand looked toward the bar for me. I waved her over and she smiled and walked toward us, stopping to shake a few hands, hug a few people, and declining a few invites to stop and visit as she made her excuses and pointed me out to her friends.

When she reached my side, I got up and gave her the barstool, then stood between her and Rick. "Here, sit down. You can have my place," he said.

"Naw, thanks. I've been sitting for twelve hours. Need to get out there on the beach and walk."

"Well, let's go then," he said. "I'm ready."

"Let me get Georgette one of those frozen daiquiris he keeps mixing in that blender, then we can hit the beach."

"Georgette," he leaned toward her. "You may not remember me. Rick. Ricky Wagner."

Georgette smiled and tilted her head as though she couldn't place him.

"Student Council? The track team?" he said.

"Sure, Rick. Of course I remember you. Sorry to be so slow. I'm tired from that long drive. Where are you living now?"

"I'm back here. Just got back. Was in Macon for years, but Shelly and I got a divorce and I missed the beach and the sailing so I'm back now. But maybe not for long. It's too damn congested around here anymore. Not like the old days, huh, Georgette?"

The barkeep swooped a cardboard coaster with a palm tree logo on it down onto the bar and slid a giant frosted daiquiri toward her. "Same room bill," I told him, and bring us two more Buds here please."

"This has to be my last one though," Rick said. "I don't want to get loaded before the cocktail party even begins."

"We've still got a couple of hours," Georgette said looking at her watch.

"Rick was just telling me about the old murder case back when you all were in school."

Georgette held her drink with both hands, and was about to take a careful sip from the large stemmed glass, but paused with the glass almost to her lips, closed her eyes, and then taking a deep breath, went on and took a few sips of the daiquiri.

She frowned, "That is delicious, but so cold it went right to my head." She took another sip, then carefully set it back down onto the coaster.

"That's some story Rick was telling. I never heard that before," I said.

"What? Oh, you mean about Myron? Yes." She took a deep breath and looked out over the pool scene. "Looks like they have quite a crowd here for the weekend."

"Georgette. Look over there. Do you recognize her?" Rick said, pointing toward Daphne.

Georgette shielded her eyes with her hand and looked where he was pointing.

"The woman in the black bikini over there? The black hat? Don't you know who that is?"

"You mean the one with the hat covering her face and the band-aid bikini? No, can't tell who that is."

"It's Daphne. Daphne Sawyer. Can you believe it? She looks great, huh? Always did and I guess she always will."

Georgette looked back at her drink. "I haven't seen anybody for twenty years, Rick. Probably will need a lot of reminding tonight at the party." She held up the glass with both hands and drank.

"Daphne was Myron's girl friend. Don't you remember?" Rick watched her in surprise. "They were elected King and Queen of Prom. You gotta remember that."

"Oh, sure. Daphne." Georgette kept her eyes on her drink. "Sure, who could forget all that?"

"I want to know more about that old murder case. It interests me," I said.

She set the drink down and looked at both of us. "Did we really come all this way to talk about that horrible murder? I mean come on, guys. It's been over and done with for twenty years. We didn't come down here to rehash ancient history, did we?"

"Jeez. Sorry I brought it up. I didn't mean anything by it," Rick said, looking at me for help.

"It's okay, Rick. Georgette's just tired."

"Yeah, I didn't mean to bite your head off." She passed a hand over her eyes. "You know what? I'm seeing those lights again."

I knew what that meant. Before one of her migraines sets in, she sees strange lights, and everything suddenly looks eerie and unnatural to her. I knew it was time for her to go upstairs, take a pill, and lie down, or else she would never make it to the cocktail party that evening.

"Honey, you better get yourself back upstairs and catch a nap." I advised.

She nodded. "Dammit. I was so hoping this was not going to happen at all during this big weekend. I'll go right up and lie down. Maybe I can head it off." She looked over at Rick. "I get these migraines…"

"Oh, sorry to hear that. My mother used to get those. I know all about what a pain in the ass they are." He winced. "Sorry for the language."

"Oh, I've heard it all before," she smiled. "I cuss with the best of them, don't worry." She left half the daiquiri and stood. "You two go walk the beach and I'll be upstairs." I put my arm around her and gave her a kiss on the forehead before she started back.

"You know what?" Rick said as soon as she left. "The hell with it. Changed my mind. Let's have another one after all," and he signaled the bartender for two more Buds.

# 3

# THE COCKTAIL PARTY

By lying down and taking the meds early on, Georgette managed to bypass a severe headache and we both took a hot shower and dressed for the cocktail party. She wore a soft blue wraparound silk dress and shawl and I even shrugged on a jacket for the occasion.

"You look very handsome," she said, as she took my arm on the way down in the elevator. "My classmates will take one look at you and eat their hearts out."

"You're the one they'll be looking at. Very eye-catching tonight."

There was a great deal of movement in the lobby as people trailed off toward a hallway far to the right. We followed along until we came to a free-standing sign in front of a banquet room indicating the Bonita City High School Class Reunion. There was a table by the door and a smiling woman seated there asked us to sign in and write our names with felt tip pens on name tags.

"I'm not putting that on my silk dress. It might mark it." Georgette stuck it on the shawl that draped over one shoulder.

I slapped the name tag on the lapel of my jacket and we went on inside the already noisy room. People were milling around the bar and many had already found their old friends at tables around the perimeter of the room and formed various clusters as they laughed and caught up with one another.

"Georgette, here. Over here." We made our way toward a table to the side of the crush of people and there was the friend who had talked her into driving down.

"Mallory!" Georgette went over to her, leaned over and hugged her friend. "Look. This is my husband, Mallory. This is Edmond Dantés Mallet. Edmond, meet Mallory Jenks."

Mallory was a beautiful woman in a low-cut dress that revealed plenty of her outstanding figure. She smiled and held out her hand. "So very glad you brought her all this way so we could see her, Edmond, and it's really great to meet you after all these years of hearing about you."

"And the same to you," I said. "I was glad to bring her over for this." Ah, those little social lies that make the world go round.

"My husband, C.J., is over there at the bar. He'll probably stay over there. See? He's the brute with the gold jacket on in that circle of other big guys. See him?" She pointed in that direction, her nails long

and bright red. Each nail had some kind of spark-
ly decoration like a star on top of the polish. Her
gold bracelets jingled as she stretched out her arm.
"The men over there with him are his old wrestling
team buddies. He's a fireman…a Lieutenant now, so
don't do a double take when you see the burn scars
on his face. He went in a second-story bedroom window and rescued a little girl five years ago and has
some nasty battle scars. Go over there and introduce
yourself, Edmond. You don't want to hear us go on
and on as we play catch up on our old friends, now
do you?" She flashed me a confident smile.

"Sure," I said, "and I'll get us some drinks."

"Just ginger ale for me," Georgette said.

"And you?" I asked Mallory.

"I'm fine, thank you. I have my vodka." She
raised her drink and tilted it back and forth so the
ice cubes rattled. "See? Vodka and cranberry juice."

"You don't drink?" she asked Georgette.

"Can't with meds." Georgette said, and I left them
to their conversation and headed for C.J.'s group of
friends at the end of the bar.

It was easy to identify C.J. after what Mallory told
me. Most of the right side of his face was shiny pink
scar tissue, almost all the hair on that side of his face
was gone. and his right ear looked like a little kid
had made it out of silly putty.

"C.J.?" I asked.

He turned, then smiled and clapped me on the
back, "I bet I know who you are. Georgette's Cajun
cop. Welcome good buddy," and he introduced
me all around to his friends. "Hey fellas, this is

Georgette's husband, Edmond, from Louisiana. She disappeared on us up there so long ago, I bet you won't even recognize her. You all need to get away from all those bayous once in a while," he said to me. "Get some Florida sunshine. This here's half our high school wrestling team. We lost some of them over the years, dammit," he said frowning. "But, hey, we got to live with it. Nothing we can do about it now."

"Watch out for that guy in the blue shirt," C.J. said. "That's Pete. He's a cop like you. The only one in our gang who turned out bad."

"Takes one to know one," Pete said, shaking my hand and laughing.

"He's bad all right," said Will. "But we keep an eye on him."

Each of the rest of the men introduced themselves, and after shaking hands with all of them, and saying I'd be back later, I worked my way to the bar and ordered our drinks from one of the three bartenders handling the crowd.

A blonde bartender with white tuxedo shirt and black skirt brought me the drinks and I signed the room check, and worked my way back to our table.

"Oh, my God!" Mallory said, as I walked up. She was watching the entrance. "Do you realize who that is coming in now?"

"No, who is it?" Georgette asked as I set her drink in front of her.

"That's Joy and her new husband." Mallory's jaw dropped and she stared wide-eyed as the couple at the entrance paused before deciding in what direction to walk.

Mallory whispered. "Mafia guy from Woodridge, New Jersey." She shook her head. "Don't say anything. I hope they don't come over here. Look away quick."

She ducked her head and motioned for me to sit next to her by fluttering her fingers. "Quick. Start saying something about something. Anything."

"What is going on?" Georgette asked, turning her head.

"Tell you later. Just keep talking. Don't look over at them."

I know how to look at somebody without them knowing I'm looking, so I was able to see a woman with long red hair, a shiny green dress, very high heels and a clean shaven man with gray hair, white sideburns, and a tan jacket over an open-collar black shirt, tan slacks, black loafers and no socks.

They paused after making an entrance, surveyed the room, and then he whispered to her and they moved on through the crowd toward the bar.

"Thank God they didn't come over here," Mallory said.

"How did Joy ever meet a mob guy?" Georgette asked.

"Long story short. She hit some hard times and almost lost her bayfront house that had been in her family for decades. She had to take out loans on it and got behind so the bank was moving in on her. She tried to sell it fast before they took it, and the realtor brought her six good solid offers at market price, but the bank wouldn't accept any of them. The bank had their own plans for that house and kept coming back with counter offers way above market value. She lost it, fell into a deep depression, and moved to Clearwater to get away from here and nurse her wounds. She got a job as a hostess in a steakhouse he owns. They go back and forth to New Jersey where he owns another restaurant somewhere near Pt. Pleasant."

"Well good then. He probably got her mind off losing her home."

"Not so fast. There's more." Mallory took a sip of her drink and looked from Georgette to me and then back to Georgette. "Since they got married, three of the men on that bank's board have gone missing. No one's been able to find any of them and they've been investigating this for well over a year now. Within a month, two more members of that bank's board resigned and left town."

Georgette's eyes got wide. "You don't think…"

"Of course I think. But they'll never prove anything, and they'll never find those bodies. Of that C.J. and I are quite sure. Keep it to yourself though. People only talk about Joy's mob connection behind closed doors."

"Joy was Student Council President one year," Georgette said in disbelief.

"So? Joy wouldn't say shit if she had a mouthful of it, but I can see how this could happen. She's in the pits and here comes Mr. Big Shot from New Jersey to make it all go away. Can you blame her?" She batted her eyelashes, "Oh, look, honey, another

missing banker. Isn't that so weird? I wonder if somebody's killing them off one by one." She looked over
to me smiling. "Let's talk about something else before I get myself in trouble. I've always been good at
that, right, Georgette?"

C.J. made his way over then with another drink
for Mallory. He was a third again as big as I am and
remained standing by me for a few minutes. After
welcoming Georgette back to Florida, he invited me
back to his group, "Come on over and hang with us,
man."

"In a few," I said.

"Good. We'll be waiting on you."

"Look, here comes Linda." Mallory nodded toward the entrance.

"She still is the Queen, isn't she?" said Georgette.
"Still the most beautiful."

"And still married to her high school sweetheart,
Jay. He's a lawyer you know. And he does a lot of Pro
Bono work. Gave the Women's Abuse center three
nice houses he owned around town for them to use
for Safe Houses. Donated office space for them in
one of his buildings too. Does all their legal work
free and donates the legal help any of the women
may need."

"That's great. Good for Jay."

"C.J., you saw Joy and her husband come in,
right?" Mallory asked.

"Oh, yeah. Adds a little mystery to the evening,
huh?" he said, smiling at her.

"Sure does, and then some."

"What the hell? Everybody's got a story, right?" he asked, looking at me.

"Right. And some stories *so* much more dramatic and interesting than others," Mallory said.

The conversation paused then as we watched the crowd in silence for a few minutes. The crowd was well dressed and most all of them kept themselves in good shape. One woman was in a wheelchair because her leg was in a cast, but she still managed to look great in a bright red strapless dress and glittering gold jewelry.

There were a few exceptions as some had let themselves go dowdy and a few women looked matronly even though they were barely in their forties. One stout woman moved through the crowd handing out her business card with a husband half her size trailing along behind.

"Oh, Lord, there's Susan running around campaigning for City Commission. I wish she'd lay off at least here during the reunion," Mallory complained. "What a butthead. I feel sorry for that poor husband she leads around by the nose. Can't figure why Morty ever married her. She's twice as big as he is."

"Somebody had to do it," said C.J.

"And there's Timmy," said C.J. with enthusiasm. He looked at me. "See that guy over there with the long blonde hair by the door? He's a fisherman. His brother was one of the crew that went down in that fishing boat they made the movie about. You saw the movie, right?"

"Sure. One of my favorites."

"Those two brothers, they grew up here. Fourth generation fishermen. But they had to move away to get work cause the politicians around here ran off all the commercial fishermen. The charter boat captains don't like the competition. The fishermen got a really bad deal. Nasty business." C.J. rubbed his fingers together making the sign for money.

"Everything around here is about money these days. Whatever makes the tourists happy, that's what greases the wheels. It sucks, but that's the way it is. Once you sell your soul to the devil, you can never get it back."

He clapped me on the shoulder. "Come on over with us when you're ready. I'm going to go grab Timmy and take him over to my crew over there. Find out what all he's been doing up there in Pascagoula."

A few more couples made their entrance, and the noise level rose with every drink that was sold at the bar. I was beginning to feel restless as I didn't know any of these people and finished off my drink, getting ready to go join C.J. and his friends.

"Oh, look, here comes Cy. And trophy wife," Mallory said as she nudged Georgette with her elbow.

There was a long silence at the table, as the two women stared at a tall thin man and his partner, a petite young woman with shoulder length ash blonde hair wearing a body sculpting lavender dress and stiletto heels. He grabbed her arm and kept her close when she almost lost her balance on the fragile heels.

Finally Mallory spoke. "I cannot believe Cy would parade his bimbo in here knowing full well Joan is going to also be here. That's just downright cruel….and juvenile besides. But then, consider the source." She tossed her hair and sniffed in disgust. "Dickhead."

Mallory discreetly pointed to her left. "Look, Joan's right over there sitting with Gayle, Daphne, and Lanny." At a round table further toward the bar sat a group of six who watched the lawyer and his new bride move across the room. One of the friends seated with her was the sunbather Rick had pointed out to me poolside. Joan, the ex-wife glared and shot invisible arrows with her eyes as her friends stared at the couple for a few minutes before resuming their conversation. Joan, however, didn't join them, but continued to glare across the room. Finally Daphne nudged Joan and whispered something to her, probably along the lines of, *Quit staring at them.* Joan responded by finally turning her head away and re-joining their conversation.

"If looks could only kill," Mallory said, picking up her drink. "Daphne must have told her to ignore them cause she's quit staring now. But who can blame Joan for shooting knives at him? After almost twenty years of putting up with his super ego? If it was me, he'd be getting a lot more than dirty looks."

Georgette gave her a thin smile, but her expression was tight.

"Well," I said. "If you ladies will excuse me, I believe I'll go join C.J. and his friends."

"Go ahead, honey,'" Georgette said. "They'll be more fun for you than we will be with our gossip."

Mallory looked at her watch. "Ask C.J. to bring us more drinks in about twenty minutes, will you please? Tell him not to worry. My limit tonight is four. Then it's quits & we go home after that."

*Running With the Devil* was playing on the Intercom and many in the room sang along with the chorus as I left the table to cross the room to join C.J. Before I could reach his group however, I felt a tap on the shoulder. It was Ricky. "Hey, man. Come have a drink with me. I'm sitting over there." He pointed to a small table on the outskirts of the crowd.

"What you drinking?" he asked. "I'm headed for the bar. And I'm buying."

In a few minutes, we were seated at Rick's table with our drinks, and he clicked glasses with me. "Here's to you." Then he nodded toward the other side of the room. "See that guy over there with the hot blonde who's tottering around on those high heels?"

"Yes."

"You know who that is?"

"Not really."

"That's the slime ball who snookered me out of $30,000 back when $30,000 still meant something."

"What happened?"

"Development scheme. He hit people up for down payments on lots, but the whole scheme went belly up. We never got our money back. I'm not the only one. Surprised he'd show his face around here. Takes some balls."

"The development went bankrupt?"

"Yeah. Down the toilet. Got half the streets laid and some of the water lines, then he botched it, the project went belly up, and he filed for bankruptcy."

"Nothing you could do?"

"I tried. Hired a lawyer of course. He tried, but nothing came of it. The guy didn't even charge me cause he felt sorry for me. He's here too. We used to be on the track team together. He's right over there." Rick nodded toward the bar where Jay and Linda were seated, a small group of men and women standing around them.

"I heard about him. He handles the Women's Crisis Center legal work pro bono and he donated three houses to them also."

"Yep. Jay's a prince. Don't worry. He makes enough on his other clients. He's a very good lawyer."

The noise level continued to escalate, and we remained silent for a while because it was hard to talk over it. *Dirty White Boy* came on, and everybody started singing along with it, getting louder and louder. We watched the crowd, laughing at some of the men as they acted up, showing off, and reverting to their younger days. Some of the couples slow danced to *I Want to Know What Love Is.* C.J.'s wrestling buddies were laughing so hard at a joke he made that one of them spewed some of his drink, and then started coughing and choking all at the same time.

When we finished our drinks and were just rattling ice cubes, I started to rise from my chair. "I better get going, Rick. I have to take some drinks back to my wife and Mallory. See you later. Thanks for the drink."

He mock saluted me. "Later on," he said, as he drained his glass and chewed on a sliver of ice.

I stopped for a while to mess around with C.J. and his friends. After about half an hour of joking around with them, I asked what Mallory was drinking, said I'd take care of it, and worked my way up to the bar. It took a while, because half the crowd had gravitated to the bar by that time, but I was finally able to get the drinks, and carried them back to the women. They were leaning in toward one another, and Mallory was whispering something in Georgette's ear.

"What's the big secret?" I asked as I set their drinks down.

Mallory jerked up her head as she laughed. "I was just telling Georgette about our famous psychic. She flew in for this from Charleston. There she is over there." Mallory pointed to a redhead who was seated a few tables over at a big round table with five other people. "She's pretty famous. Calls herself Dagmar now, but her real name is Millie. You can call her up and get a reading over the phone if you have the bucks to spend. She's not cheap. So last time I saw her I asked her if she's so good why can't she tell us who murdered Myron?"

"Good one, Mallory. What did she say?" I asked.

"She just looked at me like she was seeing through me. Her eyes went cold as a snake. Don't think she appreciated that." Mallory laughed, "Oh well. Like I said, my mouth is always getting me into trouble."

"You all certainly have an interesting bunch of classmates," I said.

Mallory laughed. "We sure do. That's what happens when your town happens to be a resort. It gets invaded by people from all over. Mostly Yankees though, although there's more and more Russian Mafia around also, believe it or not. One of C.J.'s friends installed a home theatre for one of them. They've been steadily moving in on the construction industry here and there around Florida."

"Seriously?" Georgette asked.

"Oh, yeah. Everybody knows that. Where ya been, girl?" She smiled at Georgette and then me. "Oh, that's right. You ran away from home and never looked back."

She nodded toward a man approaching a group of people in the middle of the floor. "Would you look at that? It's Digger," she laughed. "Remember we used to call him Digger cause his dad owned a funeral parlor? See him in the striped shirt over there talking with Pam and Dale? Remember when he stole that homeless man's corpse from the family funeral parlor and rode around town with the poor man propped up in the backseat of his car? He had him holding up a cigarette and a bottle of beer smack up against the backseat window? He even took him to the Scooter drive-in so everybody could see."

Mallory made a face. "Us girls were horrified. A lot of the boys thought it was hilarious though. Bet now that he runs the funeral parlor he'd rather nobody remembered that. No way would I let him get his hands on any of my relatives or friends. I don't care if he pretends to be an adult now."

"I do remember," said Georgette. "Only a twisted creep would do something like that. I don't care if he was just a teenager at the time."

I had to lean over the table as the noise level kept rising. "How long is this party going to last, you think?"

"We're supposed to be out of here by ten." Mallory tapped her watch.

"We've had a long drive," I told her. "You won't mind if I slip away with Georgette to our room pretty soon?"

"Really," Georgette said. "I wouldn't mind getting a good night's sleep tonight. Tomorrow is a very full day. The luncheon, and then there's the big dance tomorrow night." She turned to Mallory. "So where is Bucky anyway? His band is still playing for us at the dance, right?"

"Oh, yes. He'll be here. They're playing Greensboro tonight. Then they'll board their tour bus and drive all through the night to get here in time for the dance. We're really lucky to get him. And he wouldn't even charge us. All we have to do is pay his band members. We got off light. You have any idea what Bucky gets for one of his concerts? It's off the charts."

"He's always been a good guy," Georgette said.

"He's good people that's for sure," Mallory said.

The crowd was singing along with *Heartbreaker,* and by the time we were trying to say our goodbyes and take our leave, one of the men in the center of the room was taking off his shirt to show a circle of friends how ripped he was.

"That's Russell over there?" Georgette asked Mallory. "He used to be so fat.".

"I know," Mallory said. "Can you believe it? That's what the Marines will do for you."

By nine-thirty Georgette and I were headed up in the elevator, and I slipped my arm around her shoulders and pulled her close. She leaned her head on my shoulder as the elevator rose to our floor. When I escorted her down the hall to our room, I squeezed her hand and then opened the door with the room card.

She yawned as we approached the king bed and kicked off her shoes. Housekeeping had turned back the covers on both sides and placed a foil-wrapped chocolate on each pillow. She turned her back to me, and I unzipped her dress. As she let it slide to the floor, I said, "You know staying in hotels is supposed to be really good for people who have been married for a while."

"You mean good like this?" She turned and stood on tiptoe and kissed me on the mouth. "Really sets the mood, huh?" She smiled and continued undressing.

"You know, sweetheart, I really appreciate you bringing me to this," she said. "I guess you're probably pretty bored cause you don't know anybody, huh?" She draped the clothes over a chair.

"I thought I'd be bored, but I really like C.J. and his friends and Rick. Mallory too. But I *do* know you," I said, pulling her to me.

"You think so?" she asked, and a shadow passed over her face as she tilted her face up to kiss me again.

"It's not what you think; it's what you know," I said, as I gently lowered her onto the bed.

# 4

# THE BARN

At home we were both awake and up before six, but that morning we slept an extra hour, and then Georgette went right to the windows and pulled the cord to open the draperies. I blinked at the light, already bright even though it was only seven-thirty. Georgette made coffee for us in the little coffeemaker in the room and we drank it standing by the window buck naked, my arm around her shoulders.

The Gulf was flat and glittered in the sunlight. Gulls were flying around the beach looking for handouts and a pelican dive-bombed a fish about a hundred feet out. The white sand sparkled in the bright light and a young couple was building a sand castle with their child well back from the slow gentle waves lapping the shore.

When we finished our coffee, we took a luxurious hot shower together steaming up the bathroom so I could barely see in the mirror to shave, and then we dressed for breakfast. By the time we got to the breakfast buffet some of her classmates were already there nursing hangovers with tall glasses of iced orange juice and plenty of coffee.

We loaded up our plates with hash browns, scrambled eggs, biscuits and sausage, and ate by the window so we could see out to the Gulf. A Catamaran with a vivid orange and blue sail was passing about a hundred yards from the beach, and people ambled barefoot along the tide's edge. Some walked with eyes downcast, now and then stopping to pick up and examine a shell. Some walked with steady purpose as though it was a job and they were on the clock. An occasional jogger with dazed expression would also pass, weaving in and out of the beachcombers.

After several cups of coffee, I was ready to get out and walk on the beach myself and invited Georgette to come with me.

"Sure. I'll go upstairs and put on my bathing suit first though," she said. "I want to go home with a tan."

But right then Rick came in sporting dark glasses and after he poured himself some orange juice and a cup of coffee, he came over to our table.

"Good morning, you all," he said. "Mind if I join you? You have the best table in the room."

"Make yourself at home, Rick," Georgette said. "You can have our table. We're pretty much done here. We were headed out to walk the beach."

He settled himself and took a long drink of the juice, then smacked his lips. "I'm so thirsty today, I should have had more to drink last night," he laughed. "I stayed until the bitter end." He rubbed his forehead, shaking his head.

"Catch up with us on the beach when you're done," I said.

"Actually, I was thinking more of the Tiki Bar. A Salty Dog might cure my headache." He finished the juice and picked up the coffee cup. "I was thinking maybe I could show you around town this morning. Get out of here for a little bit. Give Georgette a chance to talk with all her friends at the pool while we're gone."

"Sounds good to me," I said. "You okay with that, Georgette?"

She placed her napkin on the table and started to rise. "That's fine. You do whatever you want." She smoothed her skirt as she circled Rick's chair. "Be sure to show him the old Spanish hotel. That's a beauty."

"Oh, that's torn down. Sorry to say."

"No way."

"Anything old around here is gone. It's all new and modern. You wouldn't know the town anymore. The train station's torn down too in case you were wondering, and the old Monroe house. And on and on. You name it, it's been torn down."

She shook her head. "I hate to hear that. Glad I left and glad I'm in Louisiana then. They save all their old buildings in Louisiana. If they can't remain where they are, they move them somewhere else." She moved away from the table and held out her hand to me. "Come on, sweetheart. Let's get some fresh air."

"We won't be long," I told Rick. "I'll meet you at the bar when we're done walking."

He nodded. "See you there."

* * *

An hour later, Rick was driving me over the bridge back to town when I asked him where the football star's murder had taken place.

"Ha," he smiled, "Got to you with that story, huh? Must be the cop in you. Can't even go on a vacation without stumbling across some true crime story." He adjusted the visor and lowered the volume on the radio.

"You can read up on it when you get home if you're still curious. All the newspaper and tabloid reports are on the Internet. Just google Myron's name or The Pitchfork Murder and Bonita City and it will all come up in many newspaper articles on-line. But some of it never was reported in the papers. My dad was friends with a deputy who told him some of the worst details of what the killer did to Myron. Trust me, you don't want to hear it. Don't even know if the barn's still there. So much crazy development around here. We can go check it out if you want, and see if it's still standing."

"I'd like to see it." He worked his way into a long line of cars on a highway leading to town.

"I'll turn off at the next exit and we'll circle the town and go straight out east." When he'd driven around the town and headed inland, we passed miles of endless dense housing developments and two sprawling shopping centers sandwiched into the mix.

"Your town is packed tighter than sardines," I said.

"Damn Yankees. Took it over. There're so many of them down here, there can't be many left up North. You should have seen this before. All celery fields, citrus groves, some cattle. Beautiful. Now it's a maze of cookie cutter cement block houses."

"You think you're going to be able to find the barn?"

"Maybe. Not too much further as I remember."

After a few more miles, he slowed and peered through the windshield to the right. "Keep your eye out over there somewhere. Look for a wooden barn. It used to be red. No telling what it looks like now."

We passed a small duplex with an insurance office on one side and a real estate office on the other. The car behind us beeped at Rick, and he shot him a bird and slowed down even more. "Keep looking about a hundred feet back from the road. It's around here somewhere."

We passed a two-story cement block apartment building and a small pharmacy and then he signaled a right turn. "There! There it is. Damn. We found it."

He pulled off into a circular gravel driveway and braked next to two mailboxes on posts. A portable sign near the highway read: *The Farmhouse Gifts & Antiques*. Set back about one hundred feet from the road was a frame farmhouse converted to a store

with two bay windows displaying some of the antiques for sale.

"I'll park and we can go ask them about the
barn." He eased the car into a parking space near
the building, and we crunched across the gravel and
crossed to the flower-lined path leading to the front
steps. The door was painted a glossy black and as we
entered, a bell over the doorway clanged, and the
smell of roses and cloves inside was strong enough
to make me sneeze.

"Hello and welcome," said a young woman
in overalls coming to greet us from the rear of
the store. She wiped her hands on the bib of the
denim.

"Hello," Rick said. "We were looking for the people who used to live here. The Millers."

"Oh, yes. They sold this place a long time ago.
My parents bought it. Now it's mine, and I live in the
back and run the store out of the front." As she came
closer, she held out her hand. "My name is Mary Lou
Farris. How do you do?"

Rick shook her hand. "Rick Wagner and this
is my friend all the way from Louisiana, Edmond
Dantés....uh..." he looked at me for help.

"Mallet," I added. "Edmond Mallet."

We shook hands all around and then she went
behind the counter. "Look around all you want. I
have all sorts of things in here for sale."

"Well, actually, we were more interested in the
barn," Rick said.

She frowned. "The barn? Why?"

"There's a lot of history in that barn," he said.

She made a face. "There certainly is. I'd tear it down if I didn't need it for storage. Plus I refinish furniture out there." She stepped behind the counter.

"Would you mind terribly if my friend and I had a look? Myron Miller was a friend of mine in high school."

Her expression changed. "Oh, I'm so sorry. So tragic. It must have been terrible for you."

"Yes, ma'am. Terrible for all of his classmates. Believe me. Most of us are still not really over it yet."

"Some things you never get over," she said. "And they never found who did it."

"Nope. Never did."

"It would give some closure to the family at least."

"And closure to us…his friends. Many of us are still hoping even all these years later." Rick pulled his wallet from his back pocket, removed a business card, and handed it across the counter to her. "I'm a sporting goods salesman. I cover central Florida and the Gulf coast."

She glanced at the card, then slipped it into her bib pocket. "I'll let you know if I need anything like that," she smiled. "But I stay too busy to engage in sports. My work is never done around here. But about the barn….gives me the creeps still when I'm back there working. I never, ever go back there at night," she said and shivered. "Sometimes at night I wonder about ghosts in the barn when I'm trying to go to sleep, and that's why my Collie sleeps in the bedroom with me."

"Would it be okay if we just took a minute to walk back there? We won't bother anything. I just want to show my friend. Actually, he's a policeman visiting from Louisiana, and he's taken an interest in the case."

"Oh," she said brightening. "A real cop? Then, sure. I guess I could let you all at least see inside the barn." She came back from around the counter. "They never closed the investigation you know. It's still open. My parents bought this place over a dozen years ago and people were still driving by and staring at the barn when they bought it. Some even sneaked up to steal pieces of loose siding. Daddy had a couple of people arrested for vandalism."

"I'm not surprised," Rick said. "The town was really worked up about it."

"Yes, well, as long as you're going back there, you could also help me bring a bureau I just refinished back up here to the shop if you don't mind."

"Sure," said Rick. "No problem."

"Follow me, then," she said, and she took us out through the store and into a back room lined with shelves of china, folded fabrics, lamps and figurines. Various stray pieces of furniture crowded the rest of the room. She opened the rear door and we followed her across an expanse of closely mowed grass and a few grapefruit trees toward the bare clearing around the barn.

The barn was large with the double doors of the hayloft wide open and two bays on either side of the main structure. She led us down the breezeway past four horse stalls on one side of the central aisle and two doors leading to storerooms on the other side of the passageway.

She stopped in front of a closed door and took a deep breath, then she pointed at the door without speaking.

"So this is where it happened?" asked Rick.

She nodded, still not speaking and slowly dropped her hand. She looked sorrowful as if the murder scene weighed heavily on her, and she lowered her head.

Rick and I stared at the door. There were gouges and some splintering halfway up the vertical planks that may have been caused by the tines of the pitchfork.

No one spoke for a few minutes as we stared at the door. I winced as I visualized the young man in his prime hanging there skewered, with the blood that must have drenched the door and the dirt floor beneath his tortured dying body.

"Do you mind if I see what's behind this door?" I asked.

"No, you can open it and look inside. It's just a big storage room."

I opened the door and peered into the shadowy interior. The room had a high ceiling with a stack of old boards lining one wall and chairs and tables stacked against the back wall. A few streaks of daylight filtered through a partially shuttered window in the rear wall of the barn.

"I'm sorry, but this gives me the willies. Do you mind if we go get the bureau now?" Mary Lou asked. She turned away from the spot and headed toward the next room down the passageway.

I closed the door and peered at the rafters where a hen was perched, then looked all around trying to take it all in as Rick trailed after her. "Right behind you," he said, as he followed her into the next room. He jerked his head at me to let me know we'd both better follow her.

I nodded, but stayed in place until I'd surveyed the area as long as I could without irritating Mary Lou and abusing her hospitality, Finally when I'd imprinted it all on my mind, I broke away from the scene and followed them into the next room to help carry the bureau back to the shop for her.

# 5

# THE RING

By the time we got back to the Bijou Royale, it was almost time for the reunion luncheon. Georgette was in our room changing out of her bathing suit and getting ready for another shower. She already had tan lines from the time she'd spent poolside with her friends.

"Looking good," I said as I kissed her shoulder. "You've got a nice tan going there already."

"I know. Isn't it great? I better take it easy though and cover up this afternoon. Don't want to burn. Hate that feeling when your skin feels hot and tight from too much sun."

"Yeah, don't burn. We still have one more night here in the hotel room and you know what that means."

She smiled. "Yes, I do."

"And here," I handed her a small gift box. "A present for you. Rick and I did a little shopping today."

She sat on the edge of the bed. "Thank you. Let me guess. Judging by the size of the box, it's a piece of jewelry." She looked up at me. "Did I get it right?"

"Maybe."

She untied the ribbon and opened the box. "Oh, look. I love it," she said. "I'll wear it to the luncheon." She took the ruby ring out of the box and immediately slipped it on her finger.

"It's beautiful," she said, as she held out her hand to admire it. She moved her hand around to catch the light in different angles. "I love rubies."

"It's old. Maybe from the twenties or thirties. Mary Lou wasn't sure."

"Mary Lou?"

"The lady who owns the antique shop where I bought it."

"Somehow I would never think of you or Rick going to an antique shop without being dragged in." She looked up with curiosity.

"There was a little more to it than that."

"What?" She still sat on the edge of the bed, naked, hand outstretched as she admired the ring.

"I wanted to see where your classmate was murdered."

A cloud passed over her face and she lowered her hand onto the bed. "Where Myron was....."

"Yes. The story interests me, so Rick took me out there. You ever see it?"

"God," she said, giving me a disgusted look. She rose from the bed and headed for the bathroom. "That is so morbid. Why on earth would you want to go see that awful place? That's grotesque." She passed on into the bathroom, shaking her head and shut the door behind her. A few minutes more and she turned the shower on full blast. She stayed in there so long, it was like a sauna by the time she opened the door again. Steam billowed out into the room thick as fog.

She came out wrapped in the hotel terry robe, a towel turban wrapped around her head. She didn't meet my eyes as she went about dressing for the luncheon. I had changed my shirt, but nothing else and was relaxing on the small couch by the windows reading the newspaper that housekeeping had left for us.

She dressed in silence and then checked herself in the dresser mirror. "I'm sorry," she said in a low voice. "Didn't mean to sound ugly." She was carefully putting on an earring. "I love your present. Didn't mean to get all bitchy."

"Forget it."

"Myron's death upset us all…still does. Do you mind if we don't talk about it any more after this?" She picked up the other earring to put it on while watching me in the mirror.

"Fine. We won't talk about it then." I folded up the paper and laid it on the glass coffee table.

"Good."

"You never answered me though. Have you ever seen that barn?"

She stopped what she was doing and turned around. "Do I look like somebody who would drive miles to see where someone was hideously murdered? No. I would never want to do that. And you know me better than that. Now, will you give it a rest? Please?"

She turned back to the mirror and turned from side to side checking herself. "Okay. I'm ready. Do I look all right?"

"You look great, baby," I said. "Let's go eat. I'm starved."

Banquet tables had been set up in the same private room used for the cocktail party. The tables were covered with white linen and were set up so the head table was at the back of the room. In the center of the head table was a three-foot statue carved in butter surrounded with gardenias at the base. A giant movie screen had been set up in back of it.

"Look over there," Georgette said pointing. "They carved an Oscar for Connie."

"Who's Connie?"

"She was in school with us. She won an Oscar last year for film editing *Bitter Secret*. Didn't I tell you?"

"Maybe I forgot."

"Oh, yes. We are so proud of her."

"So where is she?"

"She'll be here. Probably going to seat her at the head table." Georgette held my hand and tugged me along. "Come on. Let's go find a seat."

We ended up sitting halfway down a banquet table to the far left of the room. There were still empty chairs around us as we settled into high-backed chairs. Within minutes, however, those chairs were taken, and we were surrounded by people Georgette didn't seem to know. Brief introductions took place and as more people filed into the banquet room, all the seats were quickly filled.

The wait staff, dressed in black slacks or skirts topped with white shirts rushed through the room taking orders for drinks, and others pushed carts on wheels delivering salads on glass plates. The room was bright, the overhead lighting turned up much higher than the night before, and the steady hum of conversation surrounded us as we progressed past the salads to the entrees.

"Looks good," said Georgette as we were served broiled chicken breast, stuffed baked potato, and some mixed vegetables. Being from Louisiana, it was as I expected, way too bland for me, but I was hungry and ate it all anyway.

As they rushed around clearing the plates to make way for the dessert course, a woman at the head table stood and clanged her spoon against a water glass. Half the room looked up, while some kept talking, until she rapped again and a hush came over the room.

"I am so happy to see you all enjoying yourselves," she said. "This is a big day for us. We have a star with us today. Our very own Connie Garrett. And as you all well know, Connie just won an *Oscar* for best film editor this past year."

Applause broke out throughout the room. The speaker turned toward a rather plain woman with eyeglasses and short brown hair, who remained seated a few chairs down. "And in tribute to Connie, we have our own Oscar today sculpted in butter by Arnaud, the hotel chef." She held out her hand toward the butter statue, and there was more applause as some stood trying for a better view.

"We also have a treat for you. We brought a video of Connie at the Oscars as she accepts her award for *Bitter Secret.*" The woman asked for the lights to be turned down, and as they dimmed, the video began on the big screen in back of the room. We watched as the award was announced at the Oscars and the camera focused on Connie gasping in surprise as her name was announced. She kissed the man with her and rose from her seat, then walked as if in a daydream up to the stage.

She wore an elegant long black dress and made her acknowledgements with some pauses as she apparently hadn't anticipated winning and hadn't practiced in front of the mirror as so many of her peers had done. And then she blew a kiss "to all movie fans everywhere."

As the video closed and the lights went up, Connie received a standing ovation from all of us, and then she stood as well and took a bow.

"Thank you all so much. I am so happy to be here at our reunion and see so many old friends. Thank you." Then she waved to the crowd, and sat down again.

"Isn't that wonderful?" Georgette said.

"We'll have to see the movie."

"When we get home I'll order it for us."

The desserts and coffee came out then. The wait staff brought out huge platters of chocolate cake and lemon meringue pie.

Before too long, a few began to get up and wander around the room to speak to their various friends. As we finished our dessert and coffee, I asked Georgette what she'd like to do next.

"Oh, I might take a nap for a little bit, then walk some more on the beach. What do you want to do?"

"Would you mind if I went out to the Tiki Bar and had a beer by the pool?"

"No, of course not. Go ahead and do whatever you feel like doing."

As we were getting up to leave, Mallory came over to us and hugged Georgette.

"How exciting was that video?" she asked.

"It was terrific."

"Marilyn did a great job heading up the reunion committee. That butter sculpture is beautiful. All her idea. Total surprise for Connie."

"She's done a great job."

"Definitely. It's a lot of work putting all this together. They work on it for two years. Trying to find where everyone is or has moved to, or changed addresses and phone numbers is a tedious job."

"I can imagine." Georgette raised her hand. "Look what Edmond gave me today."

Mallory took her hand and admired the ring. "It's beautiful." She held it up to the light. "You did good, Edmond. You have great taste."

Georgette gave her a small smile and released her hand. "He really does...for a cop," she laughed.

"C.J. does too....for a firefighter. Looks like we lucked out, right? They're both great in an emergency, and they both take good care of us. What more could a woman want?" Mallory smiled with satisfaction. "You coming back to the pool this afternoon?"

"Maybe. First I need a nap after all that food. I was just going up to our room for a little bit. But Edmond is going out to the Tiki Bar for a beer."

"Good. Take a nap then, and I'll see you later. Come find me."

We left the room as Mallory rejoined C.J. and we passed through the entrance at the same time as Cy, the lawyer and his new bride were also leaving.

"Well, hello, if it isn't Georgette," he said, pausing to reach out his hand to shake hers. "Good to see you."

Georgette turned her head, but kept walking and responded in a cold tone over her shoulder, "Hello, Cy."

"Hey, wait a minute, can't you? What's the rush? I want you to meet my new bride." He still held out his hand waiting to shake hers.

"Hello, Mrs. Morris," Georgette called out, waving a hand in the air, as she continued walking down the corridor to the elevators.

I looked at Cy and shrugged, shaking my head. "Hello, I'm Georgette's husband Edmond. Nice to meet you." I shook his hand and nodded to his wife. "And hello to you as well, ma'am."

"Hello. I'm Tina," she said with a little wave of her hand.

"So what's wrong with Georgette?" Cy asked.

I shook my head. "I have no idea. But I better go catch up with her. Good to meet you," I said, as I turned to follow Georgette down the carpeted hallway.

# 6

# THE MUSCLE CARS

Once Georgette had kicked off her shoes, taken off her dress and put on a robe, she stretched out on the bed and I rubbed her back for a few minutes before leaving her to go down to the Tiki Bar.

"How come you gave that Cy guy and his wife the brush off?" I asked.

"I'm not good at pretending I like someone when I don't," she murmured into the pillow.

"I've never seen you do that to anyone before."

"Don't worry, he'll get over it." Her voice was drowsy.

"You falling asleep yet?" I asked.

"Mmm."

"See you in a bit." I left her to her nap then and went on down to the Tiki Bar. As I walked through the pool area, I saw a few people I recognized from the luncheon crowd already on lounges in their bathing suits, glistening with suntan lotion.

Some people were treading water at the edge of the pool and a few were swimming laps. Most of them were at the bar, and I took a seat at the end closest to the beach and ordered a beer.

Cy, the lawyer Georgette had turned her back on came out of the pool entrance by himself and sauntered over to the bar. When he saw me, he paused and then took a seat beside me. "You don't mind?"

"Course not," I said.

He ordered a beer and rotated the bar stool so he could lean his elbows on the bar and watch the pool. "You ever find out what happened back there?"

"Like how?"

"I mean why Georgette gave me the brush off. Is she mad at me?"

"She wanted to take a nap. It's nothing really."

"I haven't seen her for over twenty years. I can't think of anything I ever did to her to cause her to blow me off like that."

"Forget about it. Like I said, she was headed upstairs."

He went on like I hadn't said anything. "We used to go out, you know. Back in the day." His beer arrived & he scribbled his name on the guest check.

"I didn't know, but what of it?"

"I can't figure why she'd act like that is all."

I ignored him then and aimlessly watched a few people swimming leisurely laps.

"Well, okay. I can take a hint. I'll give it a rest." He took a pull on his beer and smacked his lips. "Say, do you like vintage cars?"

"Sure. Doesn't everybody?"

"Yeah?" He smiled. "I figured you for someone who would."

"I'm restoring a `66 Mustang back home in my garage. Little by little."

"It's a labor of love, huh?"

"Yep."

A teenager pushed his buddy into the pool, then cannonballed in after him, making a huge splash. Some people yelled at him for doing it, including a woman sitting on the edge of the pool dangling her legs in the water who kicked water back at him. "You got my hair wet, you little jerk."

"Say, I have to run back to the house for some things Tina wants me to bring back for her for the dance tonight. She's getting her hair done right now in the hotel salon. You want to take a drive into town with me? See my car collection? It's a sight you won't forget. All muscle cars. Every one. Six of them."

"Six?"

"Yes, sir. Six. Don't worry. I've had more than that. I have a guy who restores them for me. One by one. Then he takes them to car shows for me. I go along sometimes too. Whenever I'm talked into selling one, then there's room in the garage for another one to rescue and restore. Been doing this for years. I keep them safe & dry in a metal building I had built for them all." He looked at his watch. "We'll be back in about an hour. You want to go?"

"Yeah, sure. Why not? I'll just go to our room and leave a note for Georgette for when she wakes up from her nap."

"I'll bet you could use a break from seeing all these people you don't know, huh?" He stood. "I know how that feels. Been there, done that at a wedding up in Ft. Payne with Tina's friends and relatives. Got stuck there for three days. Food was good though. Her people can really cook. Meet me out front. I'll have the valet bring the car around."

\* \* \*

As we crossed the bridge over Bonita Bay headed for town in his Lincoln, the radio playing soft rock, Cy asked, "You ever been to Bonita City before?"

"No. Except for yesterday when I drove around a little bit with a friend to find the place where your classmate was murdered."

"What classmate?"

"Myron Miller."

"My God. Myron? That was twenty years ago. How'd you hear about that? It's ancient history."

"He just happened to tell me about it."

"So you're on vacation and you want to go hunt up an old murder location? What's up with that?"

"I got interested in the story."

"You a writer or something?"

"Nope. Cop."

"Is that right?" He glanced over at me. "Didn't know that. But how could I? Like I said, haven't heard a word about Georgette or from Georgette for twenty years." He turned the volume down on the radio. "Haven't heard much about Myron for a long time either. Except his older sister wanted attention brought back to the case recently. Like in the past year or so. Wanted the whole thing replayed in the local paper. See if something new would turn up. But some lamebrain yo-yo on the County Commission put an end to that immediately."

"Why?"

"Why? Who the hell knows? Probably cause they want to turn Bonita City into La-La Land. Where nothing bad ever happens, and it's all fun and games. Trying to attract more old people with big bucks to kick back and lie on the beach til they croak from sunstroke. Makes for a good tax base. Palm Beach wannabes. A notorious murder doesn't help that La-La Land fantasy any."

We were passing a few tall white buildings at the edge of town.

"Now here you have what I call Plastic Surgeon Row." He laughed. "See, here in Bonita City you are not allowed to look old. You may be old as dirt, but you're supposed to get plastic surgery to give you that weird stretched skin look. Look at those palaces they built for their nip & tuck operations. These guys make a killing around here. Can't keep up with all the business they rake in. You should smell the dumpsters out back of those buildings. No kidding. I took a short cut through there one day. Couldn't believe what I was smelling. Must be rotting little snips of flesh."

He drove slowly through the downtown area: a long string of boutiques, art galleries, bars and restaurants and then once past all that, we headed east.

After another mile, he turned onto a paved side road. A street sign read: Tarpon Lane, and we passed a row of large two-story stucco houses with detached garages and terra cotta Mexican tile roofs. The road ran out in a cul de sac and he pulled into a paved circular driveway at the end of it.

"And we are here," he announced, pulling up to the front of the house. It also was a two-story stucco affair with detached garage and sienna tile roof. "Come on in. We'll go out back to see the cars soon as I grab a few things for Tina."

He unlocked the front door and we stepped into a spacious foyer, a staircase with wrought iron railing flush against one wall. He pointed out the archway to the living room. "Go on in there and grab us a beer, will you? There's a little fridge back of the bar. Make mine Heinekin, please. Be back in a minute."

He crossed to the carpeted stairs and headed up taking two steps at a time.

I went into the living room as directed. It was large with a red tile floor, high ceiling and exposed rafters. A white leather couch with a woven fringed throw angled across the back of it was flanked by two upholstered armchairs. Various paintings, mostly of beach scenes and water birds, hung on the white walls. I went behind the well-stocked rattan bar, found the beers and started back to the entranceway to wait for Cy to return.

After a few minutes, he hurried down the stairs, a dress folded over his arm and carrying a Macy's shopping bag. "Okay, I found the stuff Tina wants. Now I get to show off my cars. Come on." He reached for the beer I handed him, took a swig, then led me back out to the Lincoln. He carefully laid the dress on the back seat and stowed the shopping bag there also, then led the way along a brick walkway between the house and the garage toward a back terrace.

A metal building approximately seventy-five feet wide and fifty feet deep occupied a great portion of the back yard. There was no grass, just white shell covering the yard, and the landscaping included flowering bushes and a few lemon and lime trees.

There were three wide garage doors, & he clicked on a garage opener he had in his pocket as all three slowly rose to reveal six gleaming cars side by side.

"See?" He watched me for my reaction and smiled when my jaw dropped. "What'd I tell you?"

I nodded, eyes wide, and followed him inside for the tour.

"Now, that Chevelle over there? That's my newest baby. She's just come back from getting that candy apple red paint job. Look inside. Original factory console. Nice huh?" He walked between the Chevelle and a Cobra. "Now this 4-speed?" He patted the fender of the Cobra. "She might be sold already. Not sure. I have a man driving down from Jax Beach this week to see it. He's towing a trailer with him so I'm pretty sure it's a done deal. I mean who could turn this beauty down?"

"And over there? How many of those do you see anymore?" He led me to a red Challenger with black vinyl top. "Look at that upholstery. That's original. So's the dash. Isn't that incredible? It had only one owner before me, and it never spent one night outdoors and looks it. I have the original bill of sale in the glove compartment. She's show ready."

There was also a 1969 red Trans Am with spoiler, a 1969 red GTO and a 1969 Nova with a copper paint job.

"I'm impressed," I said, and I wasn't just saying that to be polite.

"Joe, that's my guy, is working on a Dodge Dart right now. Putting a Charger engine into it. We keep this show on the road. We've always got something in the works. There's a festival with a car show coming up soon that we're going to in North Florida. Up around Gainesville. There's always a festival going on somewhere in the state and many of them have car shows. Keeps us jumping."

"Your wife likes old cars?"

"She says she does to be nice. Not sure if she means it. Joan, that's my ex….she always was into it, and went along with me to all the shows, but that's another story."

I peered inside all of the cars and then he said we'd better get back to the hotel, so we left the garage and he clicked on the remote to close all the doors once more.

He crossed over to one of the trees and pulled off a handful of limes, then brought them to me. "Here, buddy. Take these back to Louisiana with you for a souvenir. Key limes. Ever had key lime pie?"

"No."

"Try it. You'll like it." He handed them off to me. "You ready?"

"Ready."

"Let's blow this joint."

And we returned to the Lincoln for the drive back to the beach. His wife called while we were on the road and he talked to her as he took the short route back, bypassing Bonita City and skipping the downtown altogether.

"Yes, baby. I have the dress and everything else you wanted in the back seat. No, I'm not alone. I brought a guy with me from the reunion. He likes vintage cars. Yes, you met him when we were leaving after lunch. No, his wife didn't come along. Look, we'll be there in a little bit. You know I don't like to drive and talk on the phone."

He finally clicked off as we were approaching the bridge across Bonita Bay.

"Glad you kept me company on this errand. I'm thinking I'll take a nap soon as we get back. Get rested up for the dance tonight. You're going to like this band that's playing for us. They're very big right now. You like country?"

"Sure."

"Bucky's really crossover. But he's gone straight to the top. And we're getting him for free….almost. But the committee is getting off light cause he's a nice guy. We used to think he was a hick back in high school, little snots that we were, but look at him now."

"He who laughs last laughs best."

"You got that right, buddy," he said, as we pulled into the hotel parking lot.

# 7

# FLARE UP

**B**y the time I got up to the room, Georgette was awake and in her bikini ready to go down to the pool and meet Mallory. Her greeting was flat and she wouldn't meet my eyes.

"All right, let's have it. What's the matter?" I asked.

"Nothing. Forget it," she said, as she picked up a bottle of suntan lotion and stowed it in a mesh bag. Then she pulled a long LSU tee shirt over the bikini and checked herself in the mirror.

"Come on, tell me what it is," I said, as she started for the door.

She stopped and turned to face me. "I can't believe you'd go off like that with someone I already told you I don't like. With all the friends you've already met that you told me you like, why would you take off with Cy?"

"Why not him? I love vintage cars and he wanted me to see his collection. He's got a big thing going on over there. You wouldn't believe how beautiful his cars are."

"It's not loyal, that's all. If I knew you didn't like somebody, I wouldn't go hang out with them."

"Aw, so what? You're making too big a deal over this. What the hell, we're probably not ever coming back over here. What's a quick trip to see a guy's vintage car collection?"

She stopped to think about what I said for a minute. "Oh, okay. I guess I'm being bitchy again. I just can't stand con men, and he's one for sure."

"Yeah, Rick told me he has pulled some slick real estate deals."

"I'm not surprised at all to hear that." Her face softened. "And I'm sorry, okay? For flying off the handle?"

"It's okay, baby. I'm just not used to seeing you angry. It doesn't happen that often. For a minute there, I was beginning to think you still carry a torch for the man."

She jerked her head back, startled, and her green eyes flashed. "What?"

"Cy told me you used to go out with him back in high school."

"Oh, that son-of-a-bitch. You mean you and he were talking about me behind my back?"

"Georgette. Chill. That's all he said. What the hell is the matter with you? Who cares anything about who you dated in high school for God's sake? Get a grip." I watched her in disbelief. This was not my wife. Some alien must have taken possession of her while my back was turned.

She firmed her lips and took a deep breath. "I'm going downstairs now to meet Mallory. It's better if we just forget about all this. You're right. Sorry one more time." She took a few steps toward me and gave me a kiss on the cheek.

"Just do me a favor and don't mention the s.o.b. again, okay?"

"Okay, okay," I said, and then she turned around and left the room. I stood there staring at the door after she closed it, wondering what the hell that had all been about.

# 8

# SLOW DANCE INTERRUPTED

Everybody was on their own for dinner that evening, and many drove into restaurants in town. We stayed though, and ate a light supper in the hotel dining room. After dinner, we went back to our room and watched the local and national news, both of us stretched out on the bed. There was no further mention of her earlier anger, and while we watched TV, I held her close, my arm around her. During commercials, I flipped through the high school annual Mallory had dropped off earlier for us.

I glanced over the class pictures quickly and complimented Georgette on how beautiful she was even back then. I found quite a few photos of Myron Miller in the *Candid Camera* section. There were a few with the football team, Myron kneeling in the front row holding his helmet, totally unaware of the grisly destiny awaiting him. There were two photos clowning at the beach with Daphne, and she was stunning even at that tender age. He showed up again in a crowd at a beach keg party, and then again in a volleyball game.

There was a snapshot of Cy in his Nova in the parking lot of the drive-in hamburger joint. There was C.J. in a group shot with the wrestling team. It was funny to see all those burly men I'd met the night before looking so young. And there was Mallory in a bikini making a sand castle with C.J. Although so young, she had already developed quite a rack, and C.J.'s eyes were not on the sand castle. There were pictures of some other classmates, proudly standing by their gleaming waxed cars. Fairly new then; collectors' items now.

"You don't seem interested much in these old pictures," I said. "How come?"

"Oh, who cares about all that? It's boring." Georgette said, keeping her eyes on the news show.

"Kind of fun to see what these people I just met looked like back then." I closed the book and placed it on the night table.

"If you say so," she said, and she rolled onto her side and worked her way over to the edge of the mattress. "I'd better get ready for the dance now."

"Yeah, me too."

\* \* \*

The soft green dress Georgette wore to the dance that night matched her eyes. She looked great, and seemed to have forgotten her anger over me going to Cy's house. Staff had lowered the lights in the room where the dance was held, and the room filled up rapidly as we waited for the band to start. A small bar had been set up in a corner of the room and drinks were being served in red paper cups.

A few workers in tee shirts and jeans crossed the stage back and forth hauling cords and checking various equipment. And then members of the band strolled on stage, took their places and tried out a few melody lines with one another.

And then the same woman who had introduced Connie and the Oscars video, stepped out on stage, picked up a mike from one of the stands and greeted the crowd.

"And now what we've all been waiting for….our hometown boy made good….*BUCKEEE HOLMES.*"

Bucky, a tall thin man with a black and silver long-sleeved snap button shirt and a Taylor guitar hanging from a wide strap, came out on stage smiling and waving a black Stetson while the crowd clapped and hollered and carried on for more than five minutes. The band played softly in the background while he made his entrance, and then he fitted the Stetson firmly back on his head, stepped up to a mike and without a word to the crowd, started right in on *Overdrive.*

The crowd recognized the song after the first two chords, cheering with catcalls and a few screams, and then settled down enough to sing along with him. They pressed up toward the stage as only a few couples hung back and watched from the middle of the room.

After the applause for *Overdrive,* he called out, "Hey, thanks you all. We're so glad to be here with you tonight in Bonita City. It's been a while. Always great to be back in the Sunshine State. Here's one I bet you all know by heart," he said, taking a few steps back, and the band immediately started in on *Meet Me Halfway.*

Some couples started dancing in the middle of the room, but most of the crowd stayed pressed three deep in front of the stage. The friends I'd met the night before were all jammed up together in that bunch. I took Georgette's hand and led her out near the dancers, and we slow danced, her head on my shoulder.

As the concert continued with more songs everyone seemed to know, more and more couples started dancing, but most of the group stayed near the stage encouraging Bucky and his band with shouts and cries of delight.

The former cheerleader, Daphne, danced close by us with a tall handsome man who held her close. She wore a skin-tight sarong dress that sparkled and glittered as she moved. She had a dreamy expression, her eyes were closed and her cheek was pressed against his chest. When the band broke into a fast shuffle: *I Think You're Putting One Over on Me,* Georgette and I left the dancers and crossed over to sit in a row of folding chairs against the wall.

Daphne and the tall man stayed together for a few fast dances. He twirled her and she moved with such grace that they looked like they'd danced together for years. Then, as they paused to catch their breath laughing, she realized she was popping out of her low-cut dress and she tugged at the material to cover herself. The band began another slow one. I looked at Georgette and she nodded, so we returned to the middle of the room, and she leaned her head against my chest once again, as we fell into an easy rhythm.

But then as we passed near to Daphne and her partner, a woman came walking fast from a group of friends sitting by the wall and before we even realized what was happening, she had flung the contents of her paper cup at them, splashing her drink all over Daphne's face and hair and the man's face as well.

Only a few dancers saw this because most eyes were on the band, but Georgette gasped, and Daphne and her partner stood stock still as they watched the woman storm away from them and on out of the room.

"What the…." I said.

Georgette mouthed the words, *"his wife."*

The man, his face showing disgust, anger, and embarrassment all at once, took his hands away from Daphne and shook his head at her in disbelief. He took a handkerchief out of his pocket and wiped her forehead with it, then brushed it over her wet blonde hair and bare shoulders and parts of her dress where the drink had made dark stains on the sleek material.

Daphne's eyes welled up with tears and then her mascara ran and she turned away from him and walked fast out of the room, the man hurrying to catch up with her. The two other couples who saw what happened, swayed in place with sympathy in their eyes as they watched them leave, then began dancing again, moving more toward the crowd at the stage.

At the end of the song, Bucky announced an intermission, and the band secured their instruments, and trailed off stage. Bucky handed the Taylor off to a guitar tech, and kneeled by the edge of the stage to sign autographs.

I took Georgette's hand and we returned to our seats. "What the hell was that?" I asked.

"That man Daphne was dancing with? Old boyfriend. Before Myron. Eric Snyder. A neighborhood thing. They grew up together."

"So what's with the wife?"

"Jealous. Made herself look like a fool."

"Too bad." I was still holding her hand.

"You'd never catch me doing something dopey like that," she said.

"Good. Then I'll go dance with Daphne."

"Ha, ha."

"They were pushing it though," I said. "He couldn't have held her any closer, and they were hip grinding."

"True. You never know what jealousy will do to a person. It can really cause some people to snap," she said. "And I have to say in her defense, Eric is such a handsome man, she probably gets a little paranoid about him. I mean he's always had those looks. Don't know how Daphne ever gave him up for Myron. Myron was good looking, but he wasn't *that* good looking. With him it was more about personality. But Eric, he could have been in the movies."

"Oh, so looks are that important to you, huh?"

She made a quick comeback. "Well, yeah, of course. Look who I'm married to."

"Nobody has ever accused me of being handsome," I said.

"Oh, but you'll do," she said, and took my hand. "Come on. Let's go get a drink. I'm thirsty."

* * *

After the flung drink episode, the parties involved never returned. We stayed another hour, then left shortly before the end of the concert. All those country songs and that slow dancing had done its work, and when we got back up to the room, we fell laughing down on the bed and I leaned over her and kissed her, and we took it from there.

We slept well, but I was awake very early. It was still dark outside, but it was predawn and I had a strong urge to waste no time getting back on the road and headed for home. I couldn't shake the feeling that we'd better hurry, so I touched Georgette on the shoulder and asked her to get up and start packing. Time we checked out. We could stop for breakfast on the way.

# 9

# BAD HOMECOMING

To alleviate the boredom of driving through the Panhandle, I mulled over what I'd learned about Myron's murder. It intrigued me enough that I couldn't stop going over and over what little I'd learned. But as soon as we arrived back at our house, late afternoon, all that changed in an instant.

The first warning I had were muddy ruts running through the front yard and toward the back yard. The front of the house looked all right as we pulled up, and all was as we had left it, but something was very wrong.

"Stay in the car," I told Georgette.

"But…"

"Stay in the car. Do what I'm telling you." I leaned across her for the glove compartment, opened it, and retrieved my revolver.

"Oh, my God," she said. "What are you doing?"

"It's nothing maybe. Just being cautious." I got out of the car and followed the muddy ruts through the wet grass. It led the hundred feet back to the outbuilding where I kept my Mustang locked up and protected from the weather. As soon as I saw the tracks going back there I knew what had happened, and continued on toward the shed, my stomach clenched. The wide door to the shed was closed, and the hasp that held it secure still had its padlock, but a closer look revealed it was not locked. The hasp had been sawed and it was repositioned so it would look still locked.

I removed it, lifted the latch off the clete and opened the plank door. My Mustang was gone. I remained standing there in disbelief like a dummy, then shaking my head to wake myself out of the trance, I hurried back to the house and checked the back door.

The door was closed, but one of the window-panes in the top half of the back kitchen door was shattered. I immediately went up the steps, opened the door and stepped inside the kitchen. At first glance it didn't look like anything was missing from there, but I knew even before I went on through the house that everything of quick turnover value would be gone.

Ice crawled up my spine as I took a quick pass through the house. Our belongings were tossed around in heaps of clothes, pots and pans, books, papers, cushions, magazines. Everything was a mess as though a high wind had whipped through the house. Of course the television and DVD players were missing; also the radios and the CD player. Stacks of DVDs, CDs, and tapes were missing. The bureau drawers were on the floor and upside down. The closets ransacked and Georgette's jewelry cases missing. The file cabinet was flipped on its side and the drawers yanked completely out and overturned on the floor.

Fortunately the laptop was safe in the trunk of the car, but the printer was gone. Even the refrigerator and freezer had been gone through, and they'd taken frozen packages of deer meat and homemade sausage that one of my hunting buddies had given us. All the cutlery from the knife drawer was gone as well.

They'd left the five hundred pound six-foot high gun safe alone though. It's a good thing we got back when we did or they might have come back with a trolley and wheeled it on out of the house and onto their pickup. My blood was running hot and I could feel it throbbing against my temples. My anger was dangerously elevated, and yet I knew I had to keep it together and go outside to bring Georgette into the house to see the aftermath of our first home invasion.

I wished I could spare her the sight of all this destruction and mess, but it had to be done, so I splashed cold water on my face to cool off. My face felt like it was on fire from all the steaming anger inside me. I looked in the mirror and it was like looking at someone else. I looked terrible. My eyes were wild and my mouth distorted. I looked away, ran my fingers through my hair, rubbed my temples and went on outside to collect my wife.

When I led her through the various rooms of the house, she was as expressionless as a zombie. She didn't cry as I expected her to, even when she saw the thieves had taken all her underwear from the bureau drawers. When I say all of it, I mean all of it. Two drawers of slips, bras, panties, stockings. all gone.

"What the *hell* do they want with my underwear?" she asked, standing in the center of our bedroom. "That is so sick." She put her hands over her face and sat down on the edge of the bed. The comforter and pillows were shoved to the far end of the mattress as though they had lifted it up to check underneath for stashed money or a pistol. The bed skirt was torn away so they had hunted under the bed as well. The only things we kept under the bed were suitcases, and we had taken two of those, so there had been only an old battered one left, but even that was gone.

She finally got up from the bed and started trudging toward the kitchen to make a pot of coffee. "I'd get us a beer, but they probably took any beer that we left here."

"There was a bottle of wine in the cabinet," I reminded her. "A glass of wine might help about now."

"I'll look." I heard her slamming the cabinet doors above and under the kitchen counter. "Nope." she called. "*Nada.*"

"Oh, wait a minute," she called a few minutes later. "I found that old bottle of tequila that we brought back from San Antonio."

"I'll be right there," I said.

When I walked into the kitchen, she was standing on a folding stepladder and holding the bottle. "I had stashed it up here beside some appliances I hardly ever use. "Look. We never even opened it."

"Well, we're opening it tonight. Bring it on down here."

So we each had a few shots of tequila and all we had for chasers was a bottle of lemon lime soda, but that was enough to get us through the shock of the burglary.

"Now that you've had a few shots to take the edge off, how are you feeling?" she asked.

"Remember that line Nick Nolte says in *Extreme Prejudice?*"

"What line?"

"The only thing that ever scared the hell out of me is myself," I said.

"That bad, huh?"

"Yep. It's that bad."

"Well, don't do anything crazy, that's all I ask. I don't want to have to visit you in jail."

"Can't do anything crazy. Don't know who did this….yet."

"Any ideas?"

"Maybe."

"Who?"

"I'm not saying anything. Don't know enough yet."

"What if it's that man who threatened you? The one who said you'd pay for shooting his brother."

"Could be. I'd have to find some evidence before jumping to that conclusion."

"Right." She looked glumly at the bottle. "One more shot and then let's start tackling this mess."

We threw down one more, sat at the kitchen table the bottle between us, and tried to settle our thoughts enough to decide how to begin the over-whelming job of calling the burglary in, sorting through what was left, assessing the losses, digging out receipts and serial numbers for the insurance company, and putting what was left back in some kind of order.

"So how do we even begin?" she asked.

"First thing for me is...finding my Mustang."

"But we have to get some sleep before we do any-thing," she said.

"You sleep. I'm going to go find my Mustang," I said, and threw down still another shot of Sauza.

"You're not leaving me here alone?"

"I'll wait until Dwight comes to make his report, then you can come with me if you want. But you'll be better off staying here and getting some sleep yourself."

"I'll be too scared to go to sleep."

"Don't worry. They got what they wanted. Why would they need to come back?"

"Leave me with a gun just the same. I want a pis-tol right by my bed, right beside the cell phone."

"And keep Hoss in the bedroom with you," I said, as I crossed to the wall phone to call the Police Station.

# 10

# STUBS

Dwight, a fellow cop, came by the house and we walked him through each room. I took him outside and showed him the tracks from the truck and the trailer that they'd used to haul away the Mustang.

"Damn, son," he said. "I'd hate to be this son of a bitch when you find him."

"Him or them, probably a them," I said.

Dwight surveyed the interior of the shed, looking all around the cement floor, and also at the rafters where various belts, cords, and coils of rope hung from nails.

"And they even stole the deer camera I had hidden in a tree near the back door. They left the camera in front alone, because they never went around there anyway."

"Too bad you didn't have one out here by the garage," Dwight said.

"I know, dammit. Hardly anyone even knew I had a car stored back here."

"We'll find whoever it was. I hope it's before he gets rid of the car though."

"I'm calling Stubs for help. He knows all the antique car dealers around."

"Sure does. And think about this," he said. "Who knew you were out of town?"

"I don't know. Stubs kept Hoss at his trailer for the weekend. I'll ask him when I find him if he told anybody."

"I'll go back and make out a report. Get a BOLO out on the Mustang. You make a list of everything you're missing. You know the drill." He clapped a hand on my shoulder as we walked out of the shed. "I'm sorry, man. That's got to be rough duty to come home to this disaster. But don't worry. St. Beatrice is a very small town and this has to be somebody we both know. We'll find him."

"Not if I find him first," I said, as I began closing the double doors again to lock up the shed.

Dwight snorted. "I know, brother, I hear you."

* * *

As soon as Dwight left, I put in an SOS call to Stubs. It only took him a few minutes to flip through his address book and give me a list of anyone he knew who either collected or bought and sold vintage cars. He also told me he said nothing to anyone about us being out of town. However, he did say he took Hoss in his pickup for rides a few times during the days we'd been away. And possibly someone who knew Hoss was our dog figured out we were gone for a while and he was dog sitting.

"Or they just could have been watching the house each time they passed and noticed how quiet it was and how the car was gone for a long time."

"We left the TV on and the radio in the kitchen. Plus I have timers on the lights."

"All they have to do is knock and when nobody answers, they see through all those tricks. They also wait around nearby to see if you have a silent alarm after they force an entry somewhere."

"I know all that, Stubs. But get this, whoever did this stole the deer camera I had out back, and it was hidden pretty damn well."

"They ain't dumb, that's for sure."

"Maybe," I said. "They might not be as smart as they think though."

"Usually aren't. Something will turn up, cousin. I'll keep my ears and my eyes open. Let me know if you need me to help. Whatever you want. I got your back."

"Thanks, Stubs." I clicked off anxious to start calling the numbers he had given me. I called numbers in Shreveport, Alexandria, Faraday, Houma, Hammond, Henderson, Breaux Bridge, Franklin and Lake Charles. The ones who answered said no, they hadn't bought any Mustangs in the last three days and hadn't been asked if they were interested in one either. I left messages for the ones who didn't answer to please call me back, and then started on the Texas numbers Stubs had given me.

I called collectors in Dime Box, Giddings, Yoakam, Corpus Cristi, and Vidor and got nowhere. But Walter Crosby in Rye turned out to be the answer to my prayers.

"Yes," Walter said. "I just bought a '66 Mustang. Picked it up in Lake Charles last night. Haven't even had a chance to go over it yet."

"Is it silver blue with blue upholstery and dash?"

"Yes."

"Mine was stolen sometime over the weekend from a locked shed." I gave him the VIN number. "They just backed a truck and trailer in while I was out of town."

"That's a lousy break," he said. "I'll go check that VIN right away. I was in a hurry to pay the man and get back to Texas and didn't pay that much attention. It was an older man and he said he was getting rid of his car collection because he had to have back surgery. I believed him and the price was low enough to make me want to hurry up and grab it. I should have been suspicious that it was hot, but the old man seemed so honest."

"A good con job," I said.

"He endorsed the back of the title. I paid him cash. He helped me load it onto my trailer and we shook hands. That was the end of it. By the time I got back to the house, I was too tired to even unload it. It's still sitting out there on the trailer in the yard. He's not the only one who is old. Me too."

"I kept a copy of the title in the glove box. But I have the original in my files that I'll bring to show you. Tell me how to get to your house and I'll drive right over with a trailer to pick it up. That be all right?"

"So if this is your car, then I'm out two thousand dollars? That would be really bad news. My wife is going to be mad as a hornet. She's always harping at me that I have enough cars as it is."

"Call your Sheriff and ask him to look it up. There's already a BOLO out on it. It will take me well over three hours to get over there by the time I find your house in the dark."

"Come on over then. I don't want to get into any trouble. I had no idea it was a hot car. He just seemed like an honest old man who was hurting. We go to bed early but I'll make some coffee and wait up for you."

"You won't get into any trouble. If we ever find the thief, he'll have to pay you restitution. I'm a cop by the way. You have my number on Caller ID if you need to call me in the meantime? After you check the VIN?"

Walter cleared his throat. "I have your number," he said, "and I'll tell you how to get here. Got a pencil?"

# 11

# RYE, TEXAS

I took the back route through Lawtell and Eunice and DeRidder, stopped for a hamburger in DeRidder, then hurried on to the Texas state line. Each time I drive over to Texas everything feels different as soon as I cross that line. It has to do with knowing I am facing almost a thousand miles of Lone Star territory ahead of me. Open spaces like nowhere I've ever been before. Louisiana has a lot of open spaces, but nothing like Texas. Texas makes me feel free in a way I don't experience anywhere else. But I was in a hurry and didn't dwell on these thoughts as I drove on into the night headed for Rye.

Rye is near the Big Thicket National Preserve woods and swamp acreage where I'd been hunting a few times with friends. I was somewhat familiar with it, so it didn't take me long to find Walter's house on a dead-end street with only a few scattered houses.

The house number was printed on luminous stickers glued to the black mailbox near the curb, and a row of small cone lights edged the cement walkway. The house had a bare look with no bushes or trees growing around the brick exterior, and a welcoming wall-mounted lantern glowed on the screen porch.

Walter opened the door before I even knocked so he had seen my headlights pull into the driveway.

"Didn't want to wake the wife," he said in a low voice. "Come on in."

Walter was well built for an older man and balding with white hair and glasses. "You made good time," he said.

"Would have been quicker but I stopped for a hamburger."

"Come on in the kitchen. My wife left you a piece of cake from dinner. She said she's sorry she couldn't stay awake this late and to please enjoy the cake she baked today."

He brought a foil wrapped dessert plate out of the refrigerator and motioned me to sit in a booth that was set in a corner of the big country kitchen. "Sit down and I'll get you a cup of coffee. She made you a fresh pot and said you'd need it for the ride back."

"That's great. Thank you." He set the plate on a plastic mat and uncovered it. "You take cream and sugar?"

"No. Just black, please."

He returned holding a cup and saucer and fork in one hand and a steaming glass pot of coffee in the other.

"This coffee will get you back to your house. We like it strong."

"That's good. I need it after what we've been through tonight."

"Never been burglarized. That's got to be rough duty."

"Hope it never happens to you. It'll make the steam come out of your ears, let me tell you."

"We have a bull dog. Elmer Fudd. He looks out for us."

"He didn't bark when I came up."

"He's sleeping in the bedroom with my wife right now. But if you'd knocked or made any noise he would have started howling like space creatures have landed."

"That's what you want."

"Hell yeah. Those cars I got back there in my garage? You gotta have a watch dog or they'll clean you out while you're away running errands. Well, I guess you found out."

"Our dog wasn't home at the time."

When I finished the dessert, I asked Walter to tell Renata how much I liked her cake, and then I let him pour me another cup while we talked about cars and the Texas drought and the price of gasoline. And then we made for the back door and Walter flicked on a pole light out back that lighted up the metal building where he stored his cars and the backyard where my Mustang was still secured to a trailer in back of his pickup.

"There she is," he said. "Yours?"

"God love you, Walter. That's my car all right."

"You're a lucky man to find her so quick."

"I sure am. I can hardly believe it myself." I felt a rush of joy and started forward toward the car. I leaned my head against the side window and breathed a great sigh of relief, smiling like a kid who just got a new ten-speed for Christmas.

"You got any idea who stole it?"

"Possibly. But proving it is going to be another matter."

"If you show me a photo of anyone you suspect, I can maybe recognize him," Walter said.

"Oh, the guy I'm thinking of would have sent someone else to Lake Charles to meet with you. He's too slick to go himself."

"Well, come on and let's get this deal closed and get her off the trailer and onto yours. I've got to get to bed. I'm wore out already from all that's been going on."

"Let's do it then."

# 12

# THE LOST EMERALD

After I returned with the Mustang and unloaded it off the trailer back into its proper home in the shed, I stood and stared at it for a while, taking in how great I felt and what a relief it was to see it back where it belonged safe and sound. I took a rag and rubbed it down for a few minutes getting rid of any road dust from the drive home, then went outside to close the double plank doors, replacing the broken padlock with a spare.

Hoss bolted from the back kitchen door, with all the energy of a thoroughbred out of the gate. He was so excited to greet me, he danced around in circles, and after I petted him we both went inside where Georgette had fixed a great dinner. The minute I stepped foot into the kitchen, I knew she'd fixed a feast. The smells from the oven told me that. She'd set the table with a checkered tablecloth and red candles and a copper bowl filled with pink roses she'd cut from the bushes in the front garden.

"Wow, you really went all out," I said, "A midnight feast."

"Celebration that you got your baby back. Plus cooking helps settle my nerves."

I went near the stove and kissed her, and she showed me what she was cooking by lifting the lids and opening the oven door. There was pot roast, gravy, real mashed potatoes, and squash from our garden that she had preserved in freezer bags from the summer's yield. She bent over to check the roast in the oven, tilted her head up and smiled, then stood and announced it was ready.

"Now you better not have filled up on junk food on the way back."

"Nope. Too anxious to get home."

"Everything went all right?" she asked, while I was washing up at the kitchen sink. She gave the mashed potatoes a last stir before serving up our dinner.

"No problem at all. He's a good man. Of course he was disappointed and he's out a lot of money."

"Probably glad you believed his story that he didn't know the car was stolen."

"No doubt. I do believe him though. Seems okay to me. He loves his cars. Has quite a few in his garage and all around the garage outside under tarps. He's an older man. He's not likely to do business with thieves."

"Well he did."

"He didn't know what he was getting into."

"I am so glad for you. And not a dent on it?"

"Not a scratch on it. At least nothing that wasn't there already."

"Did you luck out or what?"

"Thanks be to Stubs."

"Stubs called by the way. He wants you to call him back."

"He'll have to wait until we eat. I'm too hungry for any phone calls right now."

"I said you'd be very late. He said anytime would be all right. Call as late as you want he says. It's important."

She served the pot roast on a platter and placed it near my chair at the end of the table. then placed bowls of vegetables near it as well. There was even a basket of homemade glazed rolls.

"And you even baked rolls."

"That's a garlic glaze on there," she said. "I know how you love that."

"Thank you. It's great coming home to this. That was a long drive."

"We're lucky the damn thief didn't steal the Magnalite and left some of the pots and pans so I can at least cook," she said, filling our tea glasses from a misted glass pitcher.

"Let's not talk about that right now. I don't want to lose my appetite."

"Okay, sorry." I pulled out the chair for her near my place and then seated myself. I said the blessing, then carved the pot roast and served us both generous portions.

"It's great," I said after the first bite. "Just what I needed."

"You deserve it," she said.

"We both do."

We ate in silence for a while as the refrigerator hummed and Hoss watched us carefully hoping for something to fall off the table. When she reached out her hand to pick up her glass of iced tea, I noticed it.

"Did you know the emerald is missing from your ring?"

She gasped and held out her hands to see. "What? Oh, my God. No way."

Her eyes got wide and the color drained from her face. "No. It can't be."

"Take it easy, sweetheart. At least it's not your engagement ring."

"But it can't be," she said again as her face went pale.

"Don't worry. It'll be around here somewhere. I'll help you look."

She took the ring off her finger and held it closer staring at it as if the stone would somehow reappear. "It must have been loose. This setting is so old."

I watched her as she frowned and kept turning the ring around and around, not understanding the impact this had on her.

"Come on, baby. Eat your dinner. I told you we'd look for it later."

She took a deep breath and slid the ring back on her finger, then picked up her fork and pushed a bit of squash around on her plate. She finally put some on her fork then lifted it halfway to her mouth, but laid the fork back down again.

"I can't. I'm sorry, but this has ruined my appetite. Please excuse me." She got up, picked up her plate and carried it to the counter next to the sink.

"Where are you going?"

"You finish your dinner. I have to start looking wherever I've been today. I was busy for hours trying to put things away as best I could in every room of the house. I'll start looking in the bedroom." She talked fast as she crossed the long kitchen toward the hallway.

I shook my head as she left and decided to leave her alone. I was too hungry and the food was too good for me to stop eating. Besides eating everything on my plate, I went back for seconds on everything before I called it quits and went in to join her in the hunt.

By the time I caught up with her, she was on her hands and knees peering under our bed with flashlight in hand.

"Okay, I finished dinner, so where do you want me to start looking?" I asked.

A third of the comforter had slid off the bed and it muffled her voice. "The living room. I was in there a lot today."

I went back out into the hallway and toward the front of the house where an arched doorway led into the living room, keeping my eyes focused on the narrow floorboards wherever I stepped. I scanned to the left and to the right, knowing how things can bounce when they hit the floor. We normally didn't spend much time in the living room, so it usually stayed neat and clean. Since the burglars had tossed everything around, Georgette decided to start all over and create a completely different furniture arrangement while I was gone.

She'd moved the couch against an opposite wall and the armchairs along with it. She'd moved the magazine rack and the coffee table and even a bookcase. The only thing she hadn't bothered to move was an antique brass spittoon we'd found at a flea market that was strictly for show. It was under one of the sill windows beside a showy potted fern on a plant stand.

I methodically started at one corner and moved slowly around the perimeter of the room, scanning every inch of the floorboards. I even checked in the potted fern to see if it had somehow bounced into the potting soil. Then I checked around the spittoon and thought about getting our other flashlight to see into the shadows of the bowl. It was then I saw dark spittle on the sloping rim of it. And as soon as I computed what this meant, I smiled.

"Georgette," I called. "Would you come in here, please?"

She entered the room from the hallway. "You found it?"

"Not yet. But look here." I pointed to the spittoon.

"What is it?" She crossed the room to see.

"Don't touch it. Just look." She bent over to examine it.

"See anything?"

"No. What do you mean?" She squinted at it, then questioned me with her eyes.

"Somebody spit tobacco juice in it, but missed. There's still some on the rim there."

She leaned back over to see. "Oh, yes. I see what you mean."

"It wasn't you and it wasn't me, that's for damn sure."

"So, who could it be?" she asked, frowning and straightening up. "Ohhh. wait a minute. I get what you're thinking." Then she smiled too.

# 13

# BODY LANGUAGE

I carefully placed the spittoon into a cardboard box and after folding the four upper sides closed, I taped the top so there could be no accidental brushing against the spit specimen.

"I'll take this in to Chief Ira as soon as he opens up the office."

"Okay. Great. We're on the way to finding out who the rats are that broke in here."

"They thought they were so smart and even stole the deer camera. But they aren't as smart as they think."

"Thank God for that," she said. "And now I'm going back to the bedroom to find the stone from my ring."

"Can't you put that off until tomorrow? I'm about ready to watch a movie and go to sleep."

"No, I've got to keep looking. I won't be able to sleep until I find it. You go ahead if you want."

"What is so damn important about that stone? It's here somewhere. What's the rush? Leave it be for now."

She didn't answer, just turned away and left the room. I followed her out and down the hallway back to the spare bedroom. "Hey, look at me, will you?" I said to her back as she lifted a throw rug by the bed and looked under it.

"Just let me be."

I sat on the edge of the bed. "Come sit here with me for a minute. I want to talk to you." She was smoothing the fringe of the little rug with her fingers and didn't answer me.

"You know you're beginning to make me wonder what the hell is going on with that ring."

"Nothing is going on with the ring. I just want to find the stone before it's swept away somehow."

"It's not even a real stone. You told me it was a lab emerald. I'll buy you a real one if you'll just forget about it for now."

She still didn't look at me.

"Georgette," I said, my tone irritated.

"What?" She finally looked at me and sniffed, then brushed hair out of her eyes with the back of her hand.

"What is it with that ring? Who gave it to you?"

She didn't answer, instead opening a drawer in the night table to rummage around among the odd collection of mostly forgotten and unused things in there.

"Georgette, what is wrong with you? You have to talk to me." I watched her pretend to be searching for the lost stone, but her fingers were trembling and she held her back and shoulders in a rigid unnatural way.

I reached out and took her left hand. "Look at that. You're shaking. Take it easy."

"I'm all right," she insisted, pulling her hand back.

"No, you're not."

"It's just nerves from the break-in. I've never gone through anything like this," she said, still not looking at me. After pulling the drawer out as far as it would go, she was satisfied the stone was not in there, and slowly closed it.

"You're keeping something from me, and I don't like it," I said.

"You can think whatever you want. I'm going to look in the bathroom next." She turned toward the bedroom door and took a step or two toward the hallway before I caught up with her.

"Don't," I said. "Come back here." I took her hand again and led her back to the bed where I sat and pulled her down beside me. She sat stiffly, back still rigid, staring straight ahead at the opposite wall where a framed print of a deer in a woods scene hung.

"Talk to me," I said. "Tell me about that ring."

"Don't pressure me like this. Things are starting to look weird again. I don't have time to have one of those damned migraines."

"Do you want me to get you a glass of water and one of your pills?"

"Not yet. I'll be all right if you just back off."

"I'm not going to back off. I want to know what you're hiding from me about that ring."

"It's way before I met you. What do you care?"

"I care because it's upsetting you so much."

"I can handle it."

"What? What is it?" I lightly rubbed her hand trying to make the trembling stop.

"All right, how about I talk and you nod your head." I watched her carefully as I caressed her limp hand. "Someone you loved gave that ring to you. Right so far?"

She continued to stare at the wall while grinding her teeth.

"And something happened that still hurts to this day. Something that hurts so much you refuse to talk about it."

As rigid as she was, and as much as she tried to control herself, she couldn't control the way her eyes welled up with tears, so much so that a teardrop slowly spilled over and ran down her cheek. She quickly moved to wipe it away with the back of her other hand with an impatient gesture.

"And now we're getting somewhere. Finally." Seeing that I'd made a small dent in her wall, I continued keeping the pressure on her, hoping for a real breakthrough. I kept stroking the back of her hand and wrist, never taking my eyes off her.

"So you loved someone years ago, and it's history, but you kept the ring all this time because you couldn't stand to let go, even though it's been long over with. Am I getting closer to what this is all about?"

Still no answer, but her breathing changed. She was breathing twice as fast as she had been before I sat her down beside me.

"Did I get it right? Is that the way it is?"

I waited this time for something from her. It was so quiet I could hear moths batting against the porch light outside the bedroom window.

She wiped her eyes with the back of her hand again and then closed them.

"What's the matter? Do you think I'm going to be jealous about someone you knew years ago? Give me more credit than that, will you?" Feeling aggravated and frustrated, I released her hand, letting it drop into her lap. Disgusted, I stood.

"All right. The hell with it. Don't tell me. I'm going to go grab a beer. You want one?"

She shook her head, and folded her hands onto her lap, then opened her eyes. Her eyes looked out of focus like she was watching a scene from the past.

"Sorry I bothered you with it," I snapped at her. "Keep it to yourself all the hell you want." I left her there in the room and went out to the kitchen for that beer.

# 14

# CHIEF IRA

We barely spoke the rest of that evening. I watched a movie while she kept prowling around the house looking for the lost stone. Then later, I heard the medicine cabinet open in the bathroom and then the sound of water in the sink, so I figured she was taking one of her meds, but I didn't ask her about it. I was still feeling irritated, so I just kept to myself until it was time to turn in for the night.

We didn't sleep close together that night as we usually did. She kept to her side of the bed and I stayed on mine. After that long trip to Texas and back, I fell into a deep sleep and yet come morning woke up at my usual time right before the dawn. Georgette was already moving around in the kitchen, so I hurried to shower, shave and dress so I could get down to Chief Ira's office as soon as he opened up shop.

Georgette fixed a good breakfast for us as she usually did. Hash browns, eggs over easy, sausage, O.J., and coffee. We only spoke when necessary, and I told her I'd be back right after I handed the spittoon over to the Chief.

"Be careful," was all she said.

I gave her a quick light kiss on the side of her face on the way out. Usually it would have been on the mouth, but I was still aggravated from the night before.

"Keep the doors locked," I called as I left by the front door. I always said that when leaving the house, just in case she forgot, but that day I said it with more emphasis than usual.

"I will," she called back.

It was going to be a clear day. The sun was already growing brighter, and there wasn't a gray cloud in sight. The sky was blue like my Mustang and I felt better as soon as I placed the cardboard box holding the spittoon on the front seat of the pickup and got in and started the engine. Frustration from the night before quickly vanished with the fresh air and the excitement of taking the spittoon to Chief Ira. I had a good feeling about how this one slip-up on the thief's part would somehow lead to an arrest down the road. I also looked forward to telling the Chief about recovering the Mustang.

Renée was not on duty yet, and when I caught up with the Chief he was in the narrow coffee room. I held the cardboard box in front of me, as he poured a cup and beckoned me on into his office. When I was seated in front of his desk, he took a sip of coffee, set down his cup on the desk and leaned back in his chair.

"What you got there, Edmond? Must be good to get you out and about this early in the morning when you're on vacation."

I set the box on the floor beside my chair, and pointed to it. "I brought you an antique spittoon from our living room. We have never used it. Our guests have never had occasion to use it. But one of the burglars did while they were ransacking the house. There's brown spit on the rim. They halfway missed."

He nodded. "This is good. This is very good."

"And also the thieves stealing my deer camera made me think of something else that might help you."

"I'm listening."

"I'm thinking Skinny was killed because he traded info for getting out of jail so fast on his crack bust."

The Chief nodded. "I'm with you."

"And since he dealt out of his trailer and most likely had people dropping by at all hours of the night, I'm thinking he probably had a deer camera hooked up outside, him too."

The Chief nodded again and drank from his coffee.

"I'm thinking you should have someone check the trees outside of his trailer, and all the way out to the road."

The Chief tilted his head back and eyed the ceiling. "Yep. That would be the thing to do all right. Good thinking."

I took a deep breath. "Okay then, Chief. That's all I got for now. I got to get back to the house."

"Thanks, Edmond. I'll send this over to Sheriff Quebedeaux so St. Beatrice Parish can pay for the lab work. We sure can't afford it. It'll take a while, but you already know how that goes."

"Yes, I know. And the wait will be worth it if I find out who broke into our house."

"Did you ever find out who knew you were out of town for the weekend?"

"Not really. But Stubs did take Hoss out in his pickup when he ran some errands around town. Anybody who recognized my dog could figure out he was maybe watching him for me while I was out of town."

Renée stuck her head in the door. "Knock, knock, Chief."

"Come on in."

"Sorry I'm late. My car wouldn't start. Charlie had to leave his job and come bring me to work."

"No problem. Edmond just came on in and found me in the back."

"We miss you, Edmond," Renée said. "I hope this investigation doesn't drag out much longer."

"No worries. I have plenty of work to do at the house."

"I heard about your break-in. Very sorry about it," she said.

"Thank you. We're slowly getting things back to normal."

"If it was our house, Charlie would catch a stroke over it, he'd be so mad."

I laughed. "He's not alone there, but we may be on to something now."

"Good. Glad to hear it." She retreated back to the front desk.

"Keep me posted," the Chief said.

"Oh, I will, Chief. Thank you." I stood and we shook hands and then I left to return to the house. I was still feeling jumpy about leaving Georgette alone there. It comes with the aftermath of intruders breaking into your house. It definitely leaves you with a case of ragged nerves and anger so severe you think you must be sweating blood.

# 15

# A WARNING

I stopped off to pick up the few things on Georgette's list, and hurried on back to the house. When I pulled up into the driveway, I glanced over at Georgette's car as I usually do to quickly scan it, and saw something attached to the windshield wiper on the driver's side.

Holding the grocery bag, I stepped closer to see what it was, and almost dropped the bag. Something blue and folded was secured under the wiper blade. I set the grocery bag down on the hood of the car, lifted the blade and with a handkerchief from my pocket, removed the material, then stared, unbelieving. It was a pair of Georgette's silky flimsy bikini panties.

I felt blood pounding at my temples and forgetting the groceries, ran to the house, up the porch steps and crossed to the front door. I banged on the door with my fist and with the other hand mashed the doorbell.

"Hold up. I heard you," she, called from inside the house. In a few seconds, she opened the door. "Where's your key?" she asked.

"You're okay?" My face was hot with anger.

"I'm fine. What's the matter?" She opened the door wide.

"Wait. I left the groceries outside." I hurried back out and grabbed the grocery bag off the hood of her car, then returned to the house where she waited in the doorway.

"What's going on?"

"Wait. Let me put these on the kitchen table for you," I said, and led her through the living room into the kitchen. I set the bag down and turned around.

"You recognize these?" I held up the panties.

She gasped. "Where did you find those?"

"Somebody left them under the wiper blade of your car."

"Oh, my God." She reached out for them.

"Don't touch. Give me a bag and I'll drop this in. Whoever put them there no doubt wore gloves, but just in case." She went to a bag hanging on the wall where we stowed grocery bags, pulled one out, and brought it to me. I dropped the bikini in and knotted the bag shut. "I'll stash these somewhere in case the Chief wants them after I tell him what happened."

"I don't want my underwear passed around at the Cop Shop," she said.

"I know. Me either. But I have to tell him about it."

"I almost wish you wouldn't."

"Got to though." I crossed over to the coffee maker and poured a cup. "I've got to sit down and think this over. I know one thing. I'm getting you the hell out of here."

"Oh, no, I'm not leaving you." She shook her head and pressed her lips together.

"You can't stay here. It isn't safe. This is a threat."

"If I have to leave, then you have to leave, and so does Hoss."

"Just give me a few minutes to work out a game plan. I'm going out on the porch by myself. I won't be long."

"Before you go…" she said in a softer voice. "I'm sorry about last night. It's not what you think. But I can't tell you what it's all about. It would ruin our lives together."

"Damn, woman. What the hell?"

"I know it's hard for you to understand. But believe me, I would tell you if I could." She looked away. "But I can't. I *wish* I could."

I put my hands on her shoulders. "Are you in some kind of trouble that you can't tell me? When have I ever given you the idea you can't trust me with anything?"

"I do trust you. And I'm protecting what we have here."

"So you are in some kind of trouble?" I gripped her shoulders harder than I meant to. She winced.

"That hurts."

I released her shoulders. "Look. I'm going outside for a few minutes to be by myself and think this over. By the time I come back you will tell me what the hell is going on with you and that ring. If you still won't tell me, I'm going to start wondering if maybe I better pack you up and send you to your parents' house for a visit until you decide if you want to be married or not."

"Of course I want to stay married." She began putting the groceries away and threw open the refrigerator door so hard it rattled all the condiments on the door shelves. A plastic bottle of mustard tumbled out and bounced on the floor.

"Your decision. I'm not living with a woman who is in some kind of trouble and keeping it a secret."

She didn't answer me, but picked up the mustard bottle and went to the sink to rinse it off. I went out on the porch and sat on the glider. I was doubly angry. Angry about the creep handling my wife's underwear and leaving it as some kind of a threat. Frustrated and angry about my wife's secret that appeared to mean she was in some kind of trouble so bad she couldn't even talk about it.

Hoss had followed me out the door and he sat quietly by my side for a minute, then decided to keep me company on the glider. He sidled up close to me and settled himself on the cushions then joined me in staring out at the road as I mulled things over, deciding what would be my next move.

# 16

# CONFESSION

**H**oss and I stayed outside for more than an hour. After sitting for a while, we walked down the road about a mile and back. The moon was rising, and it was going to bring a lot of wildlife out hunting as full moons always do, so we would be hearing coyotes yipping and yapping as they roamed, and owls hooting as they glided overhead, and raccoons chittering, and dogs howling all through the night. I felt so frustrated I felt like howling myself, but held back as we were passing a neighbor's house and I didn't want to stir up their hounds back in the kennels.

When we entered the house, I noticed a glint at the threshold of the front door. There wedged into the side of the metal strip was the missing emerald. I retrieved it and held it up to the light. It was not damaged.

"Present for you," I said, when I found Georgette brushing her hair in her bathrobe and slippers.

"Oh, how wonderful you are," she said, eyes bright. I placed it in her palm. "I'll go first thing in the morning and have a jeweler reset it. Thank you so much."

"Sure. Glad that's over with," I said.

"Okay," she said.

"Okay?"

"Yes. Go sit down in the TV room and I'll bring you a beer. You're going to need it before you hear what I have to say."

I didn't answer, just went on into the TV room and sat on the couch waiting with a mixture of dread and anticipation.

She brought in a tray with two glasses of icy beer and set it down on the coffee table. Then she made herself comfortable on the opposite end of the couch from me and leaning her head back against the cushions stared at the ceiling.

"The only way I can do this is to just talk it out fast. Otherwise I'll change my mind, so please don't interrupt me, or I'll quit right in the middle of it. I'm only doing this because this thing is hurting our marriage."

"Okay. Spill it. I won't say a word until you're done," I promised.

"Good, not a word now. This is not easy for me. The ring. It was given to me in high school by Myron. Myron, the one who was murdered." Her voice was raspy as she went on with her story. "He had this thing going with Daphne. She was one of the people you saw at the Reunion. The pretty one who was dancing with that tall guy, Eric Snyder, when they got a drink thrown at them by his wife. Remember?"

I nodded.

"Myron and Daphne were chosen to be Prom King and Queen in our senior year. And Prom night was coming up very soon when he was murdered. Myron and Daphne were this popular great looking couple and he was a football star and going off on a football scholarship to Tallahassee, Florida State. Daphne was a cheerleader. Everything was perfect for them. Except it wasn't really. Not what it seemed anyway."

She leaned over to take a sip from her beer, then leaned back again without looking at me. "See, Myron and I were…." She pressed her lips together. "Myron and I were meeting in secret and had been for over a month. We were crazy about each other. I'd sneak out of the house late at night a couple of times a week to meet him. Usually he'd pick me up around the corner and we'd go to a private spot in the woods where we could be alone. Nobody knew." Georgette took a deep weary breath. I kept my promise and remained very quiet, very still, while the feeling of dread kept building in me.

"You remember Cy was my old boy friend in high school? Well, I kept it a secret from Cy of course, and Myron kept it a secret from Daphne. He didn't want to tell her until after Prom night since they were King and Queen. He didn't want to spoil her big night. As soon as Prom was over, he planned to break it off and go on up to Tallahassee to get a summer job before school started in the fall. I would break it off with Cy and go up there to get a summer job also, and we'd both go to school at Florida State. We just really didn't want to hurt anybody in the meantime." She stopped for a minute to take another drink, then glanced at me from the corner of her eyes for a second to see how I was taking this so far.

I remained silent, a chill coming over me as I waited. Was my wife going to tell me she killed Myron somehow? Why all this mystery and carrying on over a teenage love triangle?

"Then one night he didn't pick me up because we made a different plan. I would sneak out of the house, sneak the car out of the garage, and drive to his place where we'd hide out in the barn so we could be together. It was an adventure. He'd placed a quilt out there on some hay so we could be comfortable and have some space instead of the back seat of his car. He set a Coleman lantern on a crate by a window so the moon streamed in and it was very romantic." She paused still staring at the ceiling tiles as though she was watching a movie from the past projected up there. "It was one of those teenage things where time dragged on when we were apart and all we could think about was when we could be together again." She took a deep breath and shook her head, eyes sad.

"I sneaked out of the house, took the spare car keys from a hiding place under the car and drove out to Myron's farm. I parked to the side where there was a small grove of orange trees, and Myron was there watching for me with a flashlight. He took my hand and led me back to the barn where he showed me how he'd fixed up this makeshift bed for us in a big storeroom there. It was like playing house.

"We lay down on the quilt and talked softly, and then he asked me to marry him once we were up in Tallahassee. He held up the emerald ring in the moonlight and when I said yes, he slipped it on my finger. He said he'd buy me a real diamond ring once he was working, but the fake emerald would have to do until then, and then we started undressing to, well, you know. It was a lot different for us than the back seat of a car. Myron held me tight afterwards, and we were so happy that night as we made our plans."

Georgette's voice rasped and she paused to wipe her eyes. "We stayed in there afterwards lying together on the quilt until I got worried and said I'd better get back before anybody woke up at my house and discovered I was missing. So we got dressed and he walked me out to where he'd met me with the flashlight and I got into the car and drove away. It was on the way out that I saw the car parked near that same orange grove. I didn't think much of it at the time, and I was so preoccupied with our new plans to be married, that I was too excited to pay much attention to anything else.

"It was only the next morning when it was all over the news that Myron had been murdered... butchered would be a better word for it...that I even remembered about seeing that car nearby the night before."

I bit my tongue so I wouldn't interrupt and stop the flow of her story.

"It was a Nova. I hadn't even connected seeing a Nova with Cy, but after hearing the horrible news about the murder, I figured Cy must have gotten suspicious somehow and been keeping an eye on me. Maybe even driving by my house a few times during the night to check on me. He must have followed me out to Myron's farm. Cy must have murdered Myron in a jealous rage. I was in shock, not only that Myron was dead, but that *my* boy friend had likely been the one who murdered him. And therefore, it was me who caused Myron to be killed because I was sneaking around behind Cy's back."

She clenched her hands into fists and started talking faster, still staring at the ceiling as if I wasn't even there. "Cy and I had never been together like that. We'd always been able to hold off. Oh, if only Myron and I had waited, but we couldn't wait. We had this thing for each other. It was so intense. If only we hadn't been sneaking around. If only we hadn't kept the whole thing secret. We were trying to protect people, and we ended up getting Myron slaughtered. And that's what it was, a slaughter. You don't even know how bad it was. I can't even bring myself to tell you all of it."

She squeezed her eyes shut as though to erase the memory. Hoss snuffled in his sleep and started moving his legs back and forth like he was dreaming about chasing a rabbit.

"I was terrified to go to the police. It would kill my parents to know I had something to do with all this. That I had really caused it all by my behavior. I couldn't bring myself to tell them. The Crime Scene crew was all over that barn for days looking for clues. They sifted through everything. Every little piece of straw. Everything. It was National news for a while. It was in all those supermarket tabloids you see every time you check out at the grocery store because it was so gory…what was done to him. It was the tabloids that labeled it The Pitchfork Murder. I'd see those headlines everywhere I went, so all I wanted to do was stay home. I was terrified they'd find something I'd left behind, some clue that would lead them to me. The quilt. There must have been evidence on the quilt. Just one loose hair would be enough to put me at the scene. But there was no mention of any quilt. The killer must have taken it away with him." She pressed her hands to her face and talked through her hands, voice muffled.

"I was so afraid of being arrested for not telling them what led up to the murder, and I knew withholding evidence in a murder investigation is a felony. I kept expecting them to show up and throw me into jail because they found out about me. I was so scared I looked sick most of the time. My parents thought it was because I was so upset by my classmate's murder. Well, that part was true. And everybody else in town was upset besides me. The local gun store did a huge business as people bought pistols for home defense. We never had anything that brutal and vicious happen in our town."

She took her hands away from her face and started twisting the ring back and forth on her finger. "It dragged on and on. They hauled kids in from school down to the Sheriff's office to interview them if they were his friends, and Myron had a lot of friends. The entire football team was called in. Anything to get a lead, but not one thing came of it."

Finally I dared to say something. "And you never told anyone?"

"Never," she said.

We remained quiet for a few minutes, the only sound in the room that of Hoss snoring on his plaid dog bed on the floor. The windows were open and a light breeze lifted the thin curtains. The Rottweiler down the road barked steadily at something and then there were answering howls from other dogs all over the area.

I frowned as I considered what she told me, trying to let it all filter through my mind. "So you've been on a guilt trip all these years."

"I sure as hell have been," she said. "And that's why I left Bonita City and never wanted to go back. Too many memories. I told my parents Cy was getting too serious and I wanted to go away to school out of state instead of Tallahassee, so they sent me off to Louisiana. And that's where I stayed. Did one year at LSU and then took that job at the travel agency in New Orleans and stayed there until I met you and moved here. Then my parents moved out to Mesa, so I never had to go back to Bonita City for anything."

"And when did the migraines start?"

She thought for a while. "It was probably about the middle of my freshman year at LSU. Something like that. Can't remember for sure when they started."

"Got to be guilt."

"Probably."

"Guilt and you wouldn't forgive yourself. Punishing yourself with headaches."

"Could be. I never looked at it that way though."

"That's what it sounds like to me. You're punishing yourself because you kept it to yourself and never trusted anybody enough to tell it. Even me."

"Don't be mad. I thought you'd hate me for it."

"Now, how am I going to hate you for something you hid all these years because you were a scared teenager at the time this happened? That's crazy. Is that really what you think of me?"

"No. I'm sorry."

"Come here." I held my arms out to her and she crawled across the couch and curled up beside me as I held her close until her breathing slowed somewhat. While I held her, I reviewed everything she had told me about that night, watching it like it was a movie playing in my head.

"You sure about seeing a Nova that night?" I asked.

She nodded, the side of her face pressed against my chest. "Oh, yes, I'm sure."

"We're going to check that out," I said.

"What do you mean?" she asked, lifting her head.

"Go get us another beer. I want to run something by you."

By the time she came back into the room with two more cans of beer, I had laid out one of my vintage car magazines on the coffee table open to a middle page. I pointed to one of the car photos.

"Did the Nova look anything like that?"

"She set the beers down on the tray and peered at the photo. "Yes. That looks like it."

I smiled and picking up a can of beer, tipped my glass and slowly poured it.

"What are you smiling for?" she asked.

"That photo is a Pontiac Ventura," I said, as I raised the glass to drink.

"What? No way."

"The design was inspired by the Nova. They made it more affordable. Ready for something else?"

"What?"

"Go get me your high school yearbook and I'll show you."

After a few minutes she brought back the yearbook and gave it to me. "What are you after?"

"Just give me a minute." I flipped through the pages until I found what I was looking for. It was the *Candid Camera* spread of snapshots taking up four pages of the yearbook. I ran my finger over the pages looking for the one I wanted.

"There," I said, stopping my finger on one of the snapshots.

"What?" She leaned over to see.

"Oh, no," she said as we both looked at the photo of Eric Snyder standing proudly beside his 1979 two-door Ventura.

# 17

# THE COTTAGES

The trip back down to Florida was quite different than the first one. Georgette sat staring straight ahead, barely glancing to the left or the right to look at the scenery, mostly an endless stretch of pine trees and some hardwoods along the Interstate on the Panhandle. She was tense the entire way and frequently rubbed her hands together or fidgeted with her fingers.

I had convinced her the night before that we had to go to the Sheriff and at least tell him what she had never revealed in the past. I talked her into going back to Bonita City while I had the time off to take her and be with her, and also into letting a lawyer pave the way with the Sheriff.

"They're not likely to want to lock you up after all these years for not coming forward when you were a kid," I told her.

"But what if they do? I couldn't stand that," she pleaded.

"That's where the lawyer comes in. You'll pick a lawyer, maybe that lawyer friend from high school Mallory likes so much. What's his name? Jay? He'll set it up so you won't go in there and tell them unless you know you're not going to be arrested. See? If you do this, I believe you'll finally get rid of those damn migraines that are making you so miserable. You can get off this guilt trip you've been on for twenty years."

She had finally agreed, yet remained glum all the while we were packing up and getting ready to drive back down to Florida. Stubs had come over and picked up Hoss to take care of him while we were gone, and he agreed to keep an eye on the house. I told him we were still spooked by the burglary and we had to get out of town for a few days to settle our nerves.

Once she had the emerald reset, we hit the road. I had tried to relax her by calling out the name of each song on any Classic Rock stations I could tune into along the way. But there was no response, none of the usual joking around about how could I recognize each song so fast, etc. I always keep both hands on the wheel but every now and then I would take my right hand off and snatch up one of her hands just to squeeze it and give her some encouragement, and also to stop the endless fidgeting.

So I didn't say much, and decided to let her have her own space, but every once in a while I'd ask if she wanted to stop for a milk shake or an ice cream. She always shook her head no and kept that poker face expression, eyes straight ahead.

Finally after we turned off I-10 and made some headway south toward Bonita City, I asked her to start looking for a motel that we could stay in for however long we had to stay over to conduct her business. That beach hotel was too expensive for this return visit and our budget, so I had one of those old-fashioned motels in mind that looks like something out of Route 66.

"If we get too close to Bonita City limits, the motels will be more expensive. Maybe we can find one a few miles away. We might be here as long as a week, so what does it matter if we're in town or not?"

"Okay," she said, her voice dull. She had such low energy, not only her voice was low, but her hair looked lifeless and fell to her shoulders without any of the usual light curl or wave.

"There," she said finally, and pointed to a motel on her side that was a collection of small cottages close together in a compound.

The sign said *The Cottages* and beneath that: *Nightly or Weekly.* "This looks like it might be all right," I said. "You okay with this?"

I pulled into a shell driveway that looped around a grassy landscaped area, then parked under an overhang in front of one of the cottages that had a sign reading *Office* hanging on the door.

"You want to come in or wait?" I asked.

"You go."

I went on inside and signed the register and did the credit card routine telling the woman behind the counter that we'd probably be there for at least two days, but couldn't say yet how long our 'vacation' would be.

"Just let me know before eleven on the day you need to leave, please. Double bed okay? Or do you want twins? That's all we've got."

"Double is good."

"There's wifi in here if you need it." She nodded toward a desk with a computer and monitor on it across from the counter and next to an upholstered settee and coffee table with travel magazines on it.

"Coffee and doughnuts and fresh orange juice are put out at six. There's a coffee machine in your room if you are an early riser. There's a Waffle House half a mile down the road if you want a bigger breakfast. Laundry room is all the way at the end next to the last cottage. Ice machine there too. Your cottage will be the third one down. It's called *The Lotus.*" She recited all this in a monotone like she'd been saying it so often for years she was on automatic.

"Thanks," I said, and she gave me the old fashioned key hooked to a green plastic tag.

"You're welcome, and I hope you enjoy your stay. There are some brochures over there against the wall if you want to find some Florida attractions."

"We're all set then?" I started to turn toward the door.

"All set. There's no one on the desk after midnight, so if you need something keep that in mind, please. There's an emergency buzzer outside the office door that will wake me up. I live in the back."

I nodded and went on out to get us settled for the night.

# 18

# THE LETTERS

The cottage was homey with a queen sized bed covered with a lemon colored bedspread and matching pillows. There was a folding louvered door to the closet, and more yellow curtains at the windows. There were a few scatter rugs on the wood floor and a white rattan bureau with a rattan framed mirror across from the bed. The room had a musty smell to it so I clicked on the fan in the A/C unit under the front window and left the door open for a few minutes to get some fresh air moving.

"Not your typical motel room," I said.

"It's nice. I like it." Georgette right away started putting our clothes away into bureau drawers and hanging up clothes in the closet.

"I'm going to take a shower before we go out to eat," I said.

"Okay, but can't we just order some pizza? I don't feel like getting in the car again and going anywhere."

She held up a post card size ad with a color picture of a pizza and the number to call for delivery.

"Sure. Whatever you want," I said, happy that she liked the room and was talking again.

When I came out of a long hot shower, she was lying on the bed in her robe and flipping through a magazine. "Pizza should be here pretty soon."

"Great. You already took care of it," I said, opening a bureau drawer to find some clothes. "I had some ideas driving down here."

"What ideas?"

"Tomorrow we can write two letters."

"Letters?" She looked up.

"Right. One letter to Cy and one letter to Eric. Anonymous letters."

"And say what?" She looked alarmed and put the magazine aside.

I dropped the towel and slipped on a tee shirt and some jeans. "One of those *I know what you did* type letters. Something like: *I saw your car twenty years ago that night and I know what you did. Meet me and we'll talk.* Something like that. I haven't worked it out altogether yet."

"What?" Her eyes looked like she'd seen a ghost.

"It's great. Think about it. If one of them is innocent, he'll most likely toss it in the garbage as a crank letter. If someone is guilty......their liver will start to quiver when they read that letter."

"That's crazy," she said, and her bottom lip began to tremble.

"I don't think so. I think it will flush out the guilty one. *If* one of them is guilty."

She shook her head. "Meet me and we'll talk? That sounds dangerous."

"But here's what's so great about it. If one of them does show up at wherever we decide to meet….a public place in the daytime….then we have something to go to the Sheriff with. The way it is now, what have we got? Nothing. Just you thinking you saw a Ventura or a Nova parked off the side of the road. It doesn't prove anything at all."

She thought about this for a minute and pulled the collar of her robe tighter around her neck. "I don't know. It sounds very risky. What do you have in mind? That I sit somewhere like a decoy….waiting for somebody to show up and do something to me?"

"No, it's perfectly safe. A public place in daytime. What's he going to do? Shoot you in front of everybody? Not going to happen. Grab you and kidnap you? No way. I'll be there watching over you. Maybe even someone else can come along, someone we can trust with this story."

"I don't know," she kept shaking her head. "This story is so explosive. I can't think of anyone I could trust with it….other than you."

"Would you trust C.J. with it? He's a Lieutenant in the Fire Department after all. I mean who wouldn't trust C.J.? I would, and I've only known him for a short time. You've known him for what? A lot longer than twenty years, right?"

"Yes. I've known C.J. since I was in sixth grade."

"Do you trust him?"

"Yes, I do."

There was a knock on the door. "That's our pizza. Sleep on these ideas. We'll talk about it more in the morning. Okay?"

"Okay," she said. "I'll sleep on it. I guess I can do that much."

# 19

# THE QUEEN'S HEAD

When I woke up the next morning, Georgette was still sleeping soundly. This pleased me because I knew she needed a lot of rest from her worries, so I quietly got out of bed, dressed and went out looking for some breakfast for her, intending to bring her breakfast in bed. Down the road I found two places, the closest one looked like it was a local Mom & Pop's in the middle of a row of shops that called itself a Plaza.

I ordered two full breakfasts to go, drank coffee while the cook prepared the takeouts, then left to return to the cottage. In the bright morning sun, it was easy to read the names on front door plaques of the other cottages. *The Lime, The Mango, The Papaya, etc.* Only one guest had made an appearance; an elderly man with a walking stick who was making his way to the front office. I nodded to him as I drove slowly past and turned in to the shell covered space in front of our cottage.

Georgette was up by that time, and I heard the shower running, so I set the Styrofoam carryouts on a low coffee table in front of an armchair next to the front windows.

After a few minutes, she came out wearing a long tee shirt dress and sandals.

"Hey, I knew you were getting breakfast for us. That's really nice," she said, and crossed to the bureau to find a scarf to tie around her hair.

"Yep. Got everything I could think of. The works."

"I'll be right there. Just let me tie up my hair." She folded the scarf lengthwise a few times and then tied it to hold her hair back from her forehead.

"You look a lot better today," I said. "You needed a good night's sleep." I waited for her before opening my breakfast.

"I sure did, and now I'm hungry at last." She came over, sat in the other chair, and lifted the lid of the still steaming breakfast and unwrapped a plastic fork from its cellophane envelope. I did the same and we ate in silence until we finished almost all the food.

"I'll bet there's a stray cat out there somewhere. I'm going to sneak the rest of my toast out to that grove of trees out back of the dumpsters," she said.

"What if there's no stray cat?"

"I've never seen the motel that didn't have a few coming around," she said. "Lots of pizza boxes with leftovers in them in the dumpster out back of every motel I've ever seen."

"You had any thoughts about last night?"

She tilted her head as she closed the takeout lid. "Maybe."

"Like maybe what?"

"Well, like maybe you're right. Maybe it would be safe to set it up like you said. It doesn't seem as scary as it did last night to me. Makes me nervous, but not scared exactly."

"Good. Glad to hear it. What about C.J.? You okay with telling him and asking him to help us?"

"Why does C.J. have to help us though? I don't get that."

"Because I can't watch both entrances of any place we pick to meet. Just the front or the back. We need someone on each door."

"Oh."

"Let's say we pick a bar somewhere or a restaurant for the meeting. And you're inside the place. And I'm outside watching the front. Anybody could come in the back entrance. See?"

"I guess." She looked doubtful.

"But if C.J. was out back watching and I'm out front watching….how could anything happen that we don't see coming?"

"I guess so. I just hate to tell C.J. that horrible story. And what if he won't help us? Then he knows the story. It's so embarrassing and I'm so ashamed that I kept it a secret all these years."

"First of all C.J. is not the kind of man who will turn us down. I am a good judge of people. We're talking about a man who spends vacation time volunteering at a children's burn camp. Do you really believe he would turn us down?"

She picked up the container and stood. "No. I do not. You're right. C.J. is not that kind of guy."

"You've been brave so far. You finally told me about it, and then came all the way back down to Bonita City to do something about it. Now be brave for a little while longer and we're going to get this thing over and done with, put it on the Sheriff's lap, and get it behind us all the way back to Louisiana and home again. And I'll bet you never have another migraine again once you get all this off your chest and forgive yourself for keeping that dark secret all this time."

She walked to the door. "It's a dark secret all right."

"You were a kid. Since when do teenagers know everything? You were scared out of your mind. End of story."

"I'm going to go scoop this toast out for the strays now," she said. "I really, really want to believe you're right. No migraines ever again? Sounds like heaven to me." She went out the door and closed it quietly behind her.

By the time she returned, I'd already written a short letter in a notebook for her approval. It was short and sweet: *I know what you did. I saw your car that night. Meet me at_____ on Friday at 2:00. I'll be wearing an orange visor cap. No blackmail, just want to talk.* I didn't know where we'd set up the meeting yet, but I knew Georgette had brought an orange visor cap along.

"There was a big silver gray tomcat out back there in those trees," she said. "I knew it. Bet there are more than just one out there. He looked like he's doing all right on pizza crusts or whatever. He's wearing a collar and he wasn't afraid of me. Somebody dumped him off here probably."

"Come on over here and sit beside me. I want to show you what I wrote. See if you like it."

She sat back down in the armchair, took up the notebook and read what I'd written. "That might work," she said, and set it back down onto the table.

"All we have to do is buy some stationary at a Walgreen's and write the same letter two times. Then we mail one to Cy and one to Eric. So we need to get their addresses and then mail them overnight rate. We also need to drive around and find a place we like for the meet."

"Everybody's addresses are usually online on the Reunion web page," she said with a hint of enthusiasm to her voice. "And when we drive around looking for a place to have lunch today we can find where we want to set up the meeting. If there ever is a meeting."

"Sure. And if we eat lunch there and you like it, you may feel less uneasy about sitting there and waiting for somebody to show up on Friday."

"Sounds all right to me," she said. "But, wait a minute. Hold up. What do we do if both of them show up? I'll look like a total idiot."

"They won't both show up. If you were innocent and received an anonymous letter like that, are you going to go meet some stranger you don't even know what the hell he's talking about? No way."

She thought a minute as she leaned her head back and looked at the ceiling. "No, I sure would never do anything that risky or dumb."

"Neither of these men is dumb. Right?"

"Nope. Neither one is dumb, that's true."

"What if the innocent one brings a cop with him to see what kind of a scam this is?"

"How's he going to prove who in the crowd sent the letter?"

"That's true."

"We're just interested in which one shows up. If nobody shows, then it was a nice try, and we maybe got the whole thing wrong from the get go."

"Okay."

"After we get the letters mailed we can maybe drive around to one of those tourist attractions they have pamphlets for in the office."

"Weeki Wachee. I used to love Weeki Wachee when I was a kid," she said.

"What's that?"

"It's a beautiful place we used to go to years ago with glass-bottomed boats and they used to film "Sea Hunt" there and even a James Bond movie. No wait. That's Cypress Gardens. Weeki Wachee has mermaids. I got them mixed up. Been so long."

"Whatever you want to do is good by me."

"We need to just have some fun somewhere. Anywhere to take our mind off everything that has happened."

"Good. We could use some distraction. Just as soon as we get those letters in the mail."

# 20

# C.J.

"**Y**ou were with Myron right before he was murdered?" C.J. dropped his fork onto his plate with a clatter, then quickly picked it up again. "Say again?" He touched his bad ear lightly. "I couldn't have heard you right."

Georgette just looked at him from the opposite side of the table and sat quietly.

We were all three having lunch at an English Pub called *The Queen's Head*. We had invited C.J. to join us for lunch there after we had discovered it in a small shopping area not far from the west side of Bonita City. There were photos of the Pub sponsored soccer team on the walls, a dart game going on in the back, and a long mahogany bar that had been brought in from a torn down saloon in St. Louis. The place was dimly lighted and furnished with dark varnished tables and chairs. The bar stools were all taken and most of the tables as well. It was a popular place, the food was good, and it made Georgette comfortable enough when we had a beer there that she decided this would be as good a potential meeting place as any to mention in the exploratory letters.

"Okay then, I did hear you right." C.J. looked around for the third time making sure no one was close enough to overhear. "And you didn't tell anybody cause you were scared, right?" He picked up a copy of the letter we'd sent out to Cy and Eric without glancing at it again.

Georgette nodded briefly.

"And you saw a car parked nearby Myron's farm that night when you were going home?"

"Yes."

"And you thought it was a Nova, but now you realize how much they look like Venturas."

"Yes."

"And you suspected Cy cause you were going steady at the time and you thought maybe it was his Nova parked there that night after you heard about Myron's murder the next day?"

She nodded.

"But then when Edmond showed you the picture of a Ventura, you thought he was showing you a picture of a Nova?"

"Yes, Edmond was testing me, and I didn't pass."

C.J. rubbed his chin, glanced at the letter again, and then toward the front windows. Georgette was twisting her napkin in her lap and looking strained. I took her hand and squeezed it for encouragement.

C.J. turned his head back and looked from one to the other of us. "So you think Eric was angry enough that Myron had stolen Daphne from him, that when he found out Myron was cheating on her with you, he went totally ballistic and off his rails? That what you think?"

Georgette nodded. "Could have been the way it was. Maybe."

"Well, guess who is getting a divorce we just found out?"

"Who?" asked Georgette.

"Eric," C.J. said, squinting at us. "And guess who he's marrying next?"

"No," Georgette said, letting go of the napkin she'd been twisting and flinging up her hands.

"I kid you not." C.J. raised his right hand like a Boy Scout. "Mallory just heard about it from some friends a few days ago."

"Talk about star crossed lovers," Georgette said. "Daphne and Eric are just now getting together twenty years later?"

"Looks that way."

"This is really getting sticky now," she said.

C.J. leaned forward, "Yeah, and so you wrote Eric and you wrote Cy and now you're going to sit in here on Friday and watch and wait to see what happens next?" C.J. was holding his fork at an awkward angle, glanced down, realized this and placed it with care back onto his plate. "See if something shakes loose? That's what you got in mind?" He looked back and forth between Georgette and me.

"That's the best we can come up with so far," I said.

"Why don't you just go to the Sheriff instead of going through all that?"

"I talked Georgette into doing it this way, because we don't have anything to give them as it is. A memory of seeing a car that she's not even sure of twenty years later, what is that? But if we stir things up and maybe get a reaction, then we have something to bring to the detectives when we do go to the Law with this."

C.J. nodded, "I can see that. Makes sense."

No one spoke for a few minutes as he thought about this. A waitress wearing jeans and a tee shirt with *The Queen's Head* printed on it in glossy black letters came by to see if we wanted dessert.

"How about we skip dessert, and just bring us another round," I said.

After she moved on with our order, C.J. asked. "Okay, so where do I come in?"

I leaned my elbows on the table to get down to it. "We sent the letters overnight rate. So assuming both Eric and Cy are in town and receive the letters tomorrow, then they will have a day to decide what to do. I'm thinking anyone innocent is probably going to toss the letter in the nearest wastebasket thinking it's some crank letter, or just possibly report it to the Law. If one of these men is guilty, then that's a whole different ball game."

"Yeah, if somebody's guilty they're going to have to find out who wrote the letter."

"Right on."

"So let me guess. Georgette sits inside here. She's the bait. You are nearby, probably out in the parking lot watching and waiting. Right?"

"Exactly."

C.J. looked around and down a hallway toward the rear of the Pub to see if there was a back door visible. He smiled. "Oh, I get the game plan. I'm the dude watching from the parking lot in the back of this place. Am I a mind reader or what?"

"Great minds think alike, C.J." Georgette smiled for the first time since we began the conversation.

C.J. laughed. "Good thing I'm off Thursday and Friday. I'm going back on duty at the station soon as we're done here. I traded off some hours for a board meeting about the Burn Camp this morning and also to meet with you all. We're on twenty-four hours, and then we're off forty-eight."

"So you'll help us?" Georgette whispered.

C.J. looked surprised. "Did you really think I wouldn't?"

Tears started rolling down Georgette's cheeks. "Oh, C.J. I did worry about it, but only for a minute or two." She raised the napkin to wipe her eyes.

"Thanks, man," I said.

"Are you kidding? No way I'm missing out on this one," C.J. said, just as the waitress arrived with our beers.

# 21

# BUSTER

The next day we did the tourist thing and visited Weeki Wachee State Park, rode on the river looking at the wildlife on an open air sightseeing boat with two dozen others, all snapping pictures of the scenery. An alligator sunning on the bank made me feel right at home. Yellow belly turtles were basking in the sun on fallen branches caught in the plants at river's edge. The ride along the Weeki Wachee River was so relaxing I could see an immediate effect on Georgette's mood. The strain that had been visible on her face disappeared and she looked like her normal self once again.

After the boat ride, we disembarked with the other passengers and strolled over to watch the mermaids in their giant aquarium. These were young women with flowing long hair and mermaid fish tail costumes floating around underwater behind a giant glass window, every now and then taking a sip of air from a bubbling air hose.

Georgette smiled and took my hand. "They're just like I remembered when we used to come here when I was a teenager."

After that we crossed over to an arena and listened to the Park Ranger's talk about the various native birds and mammals he showed us, among them a red-shouldered hawk, an osprey, and a reddish brown little fox. It was a good move to go there and be out in nature. Georgette seemed to forget her fears of whatever lay ahead, and I sure wasn't going to remind her.

On the way back to the motel, we found a Mexican restaurant and finished off the day with combo platters of tamales, enchiladas, and tacos. We each had two margaritas because Georgette hadn't needed to take any meds for migraines since we left Louisiana.

That night after she'd taken some leftovers from the restaurant outside to the stray cat, she came back smiling. "I'm going to miss that cat."

"I figured as much," I muttered from the bed where I was sprawled watching a crime movie.

"Do you think we could take him back with us?" she asked, sitting on the edge of the bed.

"Not a good idea. He's doing all right here."

"But he's really sweet. He comes right up to me."

"Yeah, and what if Hoss doesn't like him and attacks him? Then what?"

"If Hoss acts up we could keep the cat in the house," she said, rubbing my arm.

"I don't like cats in the house. Cat boxes are a pain."

"Well, then we could keep the cat outside. Cats can always climb a tree," she said, rubbing my shoulder.

"You got a name for him yet?"

"I call him Buster," she said, "and he already comes when I call him by name."

I punched at the pillows, propped myself up straighter against the headboard, still watching the movie, and patted the place next to me on the bed.

"Come on over here and watch this with me. It's getting good."

She kicked off her sandals, slid over next to me, and started rubbing my neck.

"What's it about?"

"The cops think she killed her husband but she was set up."

"If you lean forward I can rub your back," she said.

I leaned forward and she twisted her body so she could work on my back. After she finished giving me a good rubdown, I slipped my arm around her, leaned back again and for the next twenty minutes we watched the movie together in silence. By the time the real murderer was found out and the widow released, it was nine o'clock.

"We better turn in. Who knows what will happen tomorrow? We need to be ready for whatever comes at us," I said.

Georgette leaned forward. "Unzip my dress, please. I want to take a long hot shower first."

"I'll take one with you," I said, unzipping her dress.

"And about the cat?" she asked, as she slid off the bed and slipped out of the dress so she was standing there in purple lace underwear.

"Very nice," I said.

"The cat?"

"No, you. I like that lace stuff."

She undid the bra and let it fall to the carpet. "What about the cat? Can we keep him?"

"Oh, we're back to that damn cat again? Sure, sure, whatever you want," I said, and reached out to grab her by the waist and pull her back onto the bed.

# 22

# STAKE OUT

The Queen's Head Pub was in a strip mall on the outskirts of Bonita City. It was sandwiched between a pizza parlor and a chain cosmetics store. A retro wooden sign was suspended from the two-foot metal roof overhang. The words *The Queen's Head* were painted in red against a black background and the black iron chains it hung from were attached to a black wrought iron bar. The sign swung slightly in a light breeze as I watched the entrance to the pub, periodically looking to the left and then to the right and around the parking lot to scan the parked vehicles and any of the mall's customers on foot.

We arrived a half hour early so Georgette could find a seat near the front window where I could find her fast if need be. She sat angled to see outside so she could keep me in view, and although I couldn't see her from outside, I knew she could see any signal I might have to give her. We prearranged the gesture I would make if I wanted her to get out of there fast, so I had at least that much of a safety factor in place. C.J. was already in the back lot sitting in his Honda, and our team was ready for whatever came next.

The lunchtime crowd had all left and it would be another three hours to Happy Hour, so we were not dealing with a crowd scene. There were maybe a dozen people inside at best, including Georgette. I settled back against the seat ready for the long haul, with a thermos of coffee beside me in case this dragged on. We were ready.

People walked up and down the sidewalk in front of the stores of the strip mall. Back home in St. Beatrice Parish, most people wore denim.... denim jeans, denim skirts, and overalls with boots. What I saw at this mall was an assortment of bright colored shirts or tee shirts, and a lot of khaki pants and shorts and sandals. I looked each person over as I stayed alert looking for Cy or Eric behind the dark glasses and the visor caps or canvas hats. I kept my eyes moving back and forth, back and forth, and also around the parking lot.

There was a man sitting in his car a few yards away, but he seemed to be waiting for someone as he read a newspaper behind the wheel. I also kept an eye on my watch and as the meeting time grew closer, I sat up straighter and looked around even harder. The two o'clock meet time came and went. I began to wonder if anything was going to come of this scheme, and as the minutes ticked off, I had a sinking feeling nothing was going to come of it.

It was probably a dumb idea, I told myself, and I answered back aloud, "Yeah, but it was worth a try."

I figured we'd give it another half hour just in case the guy got delayed, and kept amusing myself with watching people stroll by. A woman in a wheelchair passed, a serene look on her face despite the neck brace, with a shopping bag on her lap, as a man slowly pushed the chair. Then two teenage girls passed, busily texting as they walked, not looking where they were going. I saw they were about to run into the man pushing the wheelchair, and I stuck my head out the window.

"Kids, look where you're going," I called. The teenagers didn't even hear me, but the man stopped abruptly and turned his head in time to see them.

"Hey!" he yelled at them. "Hold up."

They finally heard and startled, jerked their heads up in time to see where they were headed. Without apologizing, they detoured around to the edge of the sidewalk and right away resumed texting.

While all that was going on, I almost missed a man who stopped at the window of the Pub. He was tall and wore a cap with the visor pulled down low over dark glasses. He wore a white polo shirt, khaki cargo pants and jogging shoes. He held both hands to the sides of his face to peer in the window for a moment, then abruptly turned around and started walking back the way he had come. I couldn't see his face but I needed to, so I quickly got out of the car and took off after him. He was walking fast toward the far edge of the parking lot but I managed to maneuver around him, almost brushing his shoulder as I passed by. I got a quick look at his face, saw it was Eric Snyder, so stopped him.

"Hey, didn't I see you at the Reunion last week-end?" I asked him, giving him my best friendly smile. I was close enough to smell his citrus cologne.

He turned his head and forced a smile that came out more like a smirk, but his eyes were not at all friendly. "Yes, I think I saw you there at the hotel. They told me you're Georgette's husband from over there in Louisiana. An out-of-work cop."

"You heard right. Suspended for shooting a man." I kept smiling. "You looking for somebody? I saw you at the window back there at the Pub."

He narrowed his eyes. "Just some kind of a practical joke going on. You trying to tell me you're in on it?"

"Mostly just wanted to see who showed up." I kept the broad smile on my face, hoping to keep him off balance.

"You think all this is funny, do you? Sending phony threatening letters to people like a juvenile?"

"I'm guessing by your expression, you don't think it's so funny, right?"

"Get out of my way. I've got work to do, and I don't even know what your creepy letter is all about." He spoke so forcefully I could smell the mints on his breath and the heat of his anger strengthened the cologne.

"Then why did you bother showing up today if it's only a dumb prank?"

"I didn't show up for anything. Nobody gets my attention by harassment. I just happened to have an errand here and glanced in the Pub for the hell of it."

"Nobody's harassing anybody."

His face got darker and he held his head back as he looked down his nose at me.

"It's illegal to send threatening letters. Do you really want a call from my lawyer?"

"Last I heard, it's illegal to murder people too."

He stuck out his finger six inches from my face. "You calling me a murderer now?" He glared, and his blue eyes shot knives at me.

"Only if it's true." I kept smiling.

"Quit wasting my time with your juvenile bullshit. You've got nothing on me." He turned toward the Ford extended cab pickup parked at the end of the sidewalk. A magnetic sign on the door advertised *Snyder Metal Buildings*.

"Wait."

He looked at me for a moment, shaking his head. "You and your wife are sick people. Get some therapy, why don't you?"

"Sick? You'd know something about that, wouldn't you, Eric?" I smiled again as he worked his jaw back and forth.

"You and Georgette stay away from me is the best advice I can give you," he said, as he crossed to the truck, got in and slammed the door. He continued to glare at me as he started the engine, then backed out of the parking spot and drove off.

I walked back to the Pub and went inside, blinking and trying to adjust my eyes to the dim interior after being outside in the bright Gulf Coast sunlight. Georgette was sitting at attention at the table where she remained on sentry duty. I approached the table as she looked at me raising her eyebrows in question.

"You see him?" I asked.

"Nope. No luck. Guess our little plan didn't work," she said.

"It did work. He just wanted to get a good look at whoever it was wrote him that letter."

"Who? What do you mean?"

"Eric Snyder just got a good look at you through the window. He's long gone now."

"Eric was out there looking in at me?" Her eyes opened wide and she clapped a hand to her throat.

"Sure was. Then he walked away fast, got into his company truck and took off. Call C.J. in from out back, while I get us a round of beers. Then I'll tell you both what happened when I talked with him." I looked around and signaled to the waitress and pulled out a chair.

"You talked to him?"

"Sure did. And it wasn't particularly friendly."

"Oh, no. Tell me." She grabbed my arm.

"Get C.J. in here first so I don't have to say it all over again."

She grabbed her cell phone to call him as I caught the waitress' eye and held up three fingers and Georgette's beer glass.

Inside of a minute, C. J. had come in through the back door and hustled his way over to the table. He sat down and said, "Okay. Give it. What happened?"

"Eric Snyder passed by outside, peered in the window for a minute, then turned and started walking away."

"No shit?" C.J.'s mouth hung open. "Eric showed his face here? Wow."

"Sure did. I followed him, stopped him and asked him if I hadn't seen him at the Reunion."

"Good one," C.J. said.

"He recognized me from there. Had even asked someone who the man was with Georgette."

"Oh, no," Georgette said. "Now he knows who you are too?"

"He was angry that we bothered him with such juvenile trash as this threatening letter as he called it. Wasting his time. Said we needed therapy, we didn't have anything on him, and with dirty looks, he took off in his Ford 150."

"That's it? That was the end of it?" C.J. asked.

"He did say he'd sic his lawyer on me for harassment. Said it's illegal. I told him so was murder illegal."

"Oooh, good one, what did he say then?" asked Georgette, eyes shining.

"*Now you're calling me a murderer?*" I mimicked Eric's voice. "He warned us to stay away from him."

"Did you say anything about the Ventura?" Georgette asked.

"No. We didn't get that far."

"So what conclusions have you come to after all this?" asked C.J.

"Don't know. The fact that he showed up looks suspicious but doesn't prove anything. We still don't have much to take to the Sheriff. Georgette thought she saw a Nova that night, but then she thinks maybe it could have been a Ventura? Not enough yet. So we send out a couple of letters to see if it turns up anything. Eric shows, and Cy doesn't.

Eric is angry that we bothered him with this 'phony threatening letter'. What does that prove? Exactly nothing."

"You're right, bro. Nothing at all."

"Except that it sure doesn't look good for Eric," said Georgette. "But something odd did happen right before that."

C.J. and I gave her our full attention. "What? Out with it," I said.

"A suntanned blonde teenager walked in here, looked around at everybody, then saw me, walked over toward this table and took a picture of me with his cell phone. He turned around and left before I could even ask him what he was doing."

"A teenager?" asked C.J. "His hair almost white from sun-bleach?"

"Yes."

"Bright blue and green Hawaiian shirt?"

"Yes. You saw him?"

"Sure did. He hustled out the back door and took off on a motorcycle."

"Good, I'm glad you saw him too. At first I was annoyed," Georgette said. "Then I figured maybe he was sent by one of the two men to see who wrote the letter."

"No maybe about it," I said. "Must be. Eric saw you in person. Sounds like Cy sent somebody instead of showing up himself."

C.J. nodded. "Sounds right to me. I'll buy that."

"But even if Cy wanted to know who sent the letter, and even if Eric came in person to see who wrote the letter, it still doesn't prove anything," I said.

"No, it doesn't, but it stirs the pot. So what's next?" asked C.J.

"We know where Cy's Nova is. Safe in his garage. I saw it with my own eyes. So now we've got to try to find that old Ventura."

"For what?"

"Maybe they could find something in it or on it that would implicate Eric."

"Like what? Anything by now is sure to be gone."

"Not really. They can go over it with ultraviolet and pick up on even very old blood. If he did murder Myron, he sure got blood on him and he sure left some of it in that car."

"Long shot," said Georgette.

"They can pick up anything these days. Just one hair or tiny piece of skin or dab of blood could send him away for this," said C.J.

"He's likely junked that car. It could have gone into the crusher by now," Georgette said.

"Probably not. Why crush a car you can sell piece by piece for parts, even if he didn't want to keep driving it?"

"I'm pretty sure Wayne Futch bought that Ventura off of Eric years ago," C.J. said. "He was in school with us too. Went on to become a plumber. Makes more money than any of us."

"Do you know where he is now?" I asked.

"Last I heard he started his own business somewhere around Ocala," C.J. said. "Made so much money he raises thoroughbreds up there on the side. You ever see any of those horse ranches around Ocala? It's like Louisville up there. You wouldn't believe it."

"We have to figure out how to call him," I said.

"I'll get on it. Mallory knows how to find anybody. She starts tracking people down for these reunions two years in advance. I'll call her right now."

"You didn't tell her any of this, right?"

"No. I haven't told anybody. This is way too potentially explosive to expect Mallory or anybody else to keep their mouth shut. She might call a girl friend and say, 'Now promise you will not speak about this to anybody. Nobody. Not even your husband.' You know how that goes. Before you know it, everybody in town will know about it. I'll just say I was wondering how Wayne was doing and would she please find a way I can call him. Piece of cake for Mallory." C.J. flipped open his cell phone and called home. He drummed his fingers on the table as he waited. I raised three fingers to signal for another round for our table.

"Hey, baby. What you doing? Listen, I need you to do something for me. How about seeing if you can get a phone number for Wayne Futch? I think he's in Ocala now last I heard."

"For why? Some guy I work with wants to ask him something, that's all. Where am I? Just having a beer with this guy. Can you do this for me? Call me right back when you get it, okay?"

C.J. flipped the phone closed and smiled. "Some guy I work with? Well, we *are* working together on this. Not really a lie."

"You're walking a fine line there," Georgette laughed. "Oh well, what the hell. White lies are okay for a good cause, I guess."

Our beers arrived then and we raised the icy mugs in a toast. "Here's to finding that Ventura." We clinked glasses together and settled back in our chairs waiting on Mallory to call back as we checked out an Alaskan wildlife show on a television high above the bar, each of us going over what had happened in our private thoughts.

It didn't take Mallory long. She called back within ten minutes with Wayne's number.

"Good work, baby," C.J. said, as he signaled to Georgette for a pen & wrote it down on a napkin. "Thank you, and my friend thanks you too." He closed his phone and gave me the napkin. "There you go. What did I tell you? Do I know my wife or what?"

I handed the napkin back to him. "Better you call him than me. He knows you."

"Sure. I'll do it." He opened his phone again and punched in the number, raising his eyes to the ceiling as it rang. He sat up abruptly. "Wayne? Hey. This is C.J. C.J. from high school. Yeah. I'm good, I'm good. How you doing?" C.J. made a thumbs up as they went through the polite openers. "Look, Wayne, I'm calling to see do you still have that Ventura you bought off of Eric Snyder way back?" C.J. frowned, and then signaled a thumbs down.

"Oh, yeah? Where is that? Wait a minute. Let me write that down." He made a gimme gesture for Georgette's pen again. "Yeah. okay. Right. I got that." He scribbled a few words on another napkin, then drew a line and then another line and wrote some numbers. "Okay. I got it. I'll check it out. Thanks a lot, man. I hope it's still there. Yeah, I know. Venturas are hard to find anymore. But I just happened to remember about you buying it back in the day. Glad to talk to you after all these years. Right. Will do. Mallory's fine. Thanks for asking. Later." He clicked off, laid the phone down on the table and nodded.

"He did sell it to a junk yard a few years ago. Fat Boy's out in the country somewhere east of Ocala. It's all on here." He tapped a finger on the napkin, then handed it to me.

"We're good to go then. Tomorrow good for you, or do you want me to go alone?" I asked.

"No way. I'm in on this thing all the way. I'm going with you. Meanwhile, soon as I finish this beer, I better be getting home before Mallory starts wondering if something weird is going on and starts asking questions. I'll pick you up at those cottages where you're staying in the morning. Eight o'clock good?"

# 23

# FAT BOY'S

It took us about an hour to get to Ocala and we quickly found the Exit Ramp to the turn-off road we needed to get to Fat Boy's Salvage Yard. The road we needed to find was a two-lane, and we finally spotted it off to our right past two trailer parks and acres of citrus groves. A faded metal sign with a circular pattern of B.B. holes advertised Fat Boy's at the corner of Hidden Lake Road. We turned south and drove a mile down the blacktop to a metal fence bordering the salvage yard.

The fence was constructed of close to four hundred feet of corrugated tin roofing sheets bolted horizontally to uprights. This effectively screened the entire junkyard from view. The high metal gates were open and we drove inside to a shell driveway leading to a metal building transformed into an office. C.J. parked in front of a path made up of concrete pavers leading up to the building.

Two white pit bulls came barreling out of the office door and ran to the end of the path, stopping short when a skinny man in the doorway yelled, "Snowball. Robo. Stay." He beckoned us on. "They won't hurt you."

"That's Fat Boy?" asked C.J.with his hand on the door handle. "I don't think so."

The man sauntered down the path and waited for us to get out of the car, giving a hand motion to the dogs to sit. He wore gray coveralls and while his dogs' fur was glossy clean, his own hair hung low over his ears and was badly in need of a wash.

"Hello. What you all need today?" he asked, rubbing two-day gray whiskers and moving a wad of tobacco from one side of his mouth to the other.

"You the boss?" I asked. "Cause you're definitely not Fat Boy."

"Used to be. Got sick though," he said. "Just kidding. I bought this place from a guy years go. Kept the name Fat Boy's, but my name's Felix. What you all looking for today?"

"We're looking for the '79 Ventura Wayne Futch sold you a few years ago. Do you remember the car?"

"Oh, yeah. I remember that car. Fellow bought it for parts a while back."

"You still got his name in your files there somewhere?"

His face tightened and he looked away. "Oh, I don't give out names. Wouldn't be right. My customers might not want me to."

"It's really important. Could be part of a criminal investigation," C.J. said. He pulled a black leather billfold out of his back pocket and flipped it open to show his official looking Lieutenant's I.D. from the fire station.

Felix barely glanced at it. "It wasn't stolen," he yelped. "I had the title right here in my file cabinet for a long time."

"Nope," said C.J. "Don't worry. It's not stolen."

Felix scratched his head as he thought. "The man had a funny name but I can't think of it right off. I'd have to go dig around in the office for it."

"Would you help us and do that, please?"

"I guess it would be okay then. Why don't you all walk around the lot and look at the vehicles we got? Maybe you'll find something you want to buy while I'm looking for you. The shed's unlocked. There's a lot in there to look through." He gave us a look that suggested we should find something to help him out if he was going to help us out, then made a hand signal for the dogs and they all turned around and walked back to the office.

"Let's do it then," I said, and we followed the gravel driveway to where it turned into a wide dirt path through the salvage yard. Rows of bashed in cars and dented pickups were parked on both sides of us as we took our time wandering through the wreckage.

There was a little bit of everything: Fords, Chryslers, Chevys, Plymouths, Caddys, Jeeps, and a few imports in the mix. Some still whole, some completely stripped. Hoods were raised here and there and weeds grew up around and up through the engine compartments. Yellow dandelions, thistles, clover, and plantain seed spikes thrived in the dry ground between the vehicles. Vines trailed from sagging windshields and covered the beds of pickup trucks. The further back into the salvage yard we walked, the more creeping rust had taken over the once glossy paint jobs.

A metal building halfway into the yard housed a collection of chrome bumpers leaning against a wall, engines, radiators, and stacks of wheels and transmissions. The sun was beating down on us and we slapped at a few mosquitoes as we poked around, checking things out.

"Felix hopes we buy something," said C.J. "I'm looking, but haven't seen anything I need yet." There was a metallic smell from the sun beating down on all the cars, mixed with the biting smell of old motor oil.

"Maybe something will turn up." I entered the shadowy shed and standing on the concrete floor looked around. At the back wall on metal shelving was a collection of hub caps. I looked them over, hoping to find one for backup for my Mustang. No luck there. A wooden crate on the floor was filled with various tools, such as tire irons, and an assortment of axles was stacked next to it.

"We've seen enough, you think?" I asked C.J.

"Yeah, let's start back. He might have found it by now."

We started back to the office, passing an LTD with a front end so crumpled it made me wince.

"We didn't find anything to buy from Felix. He's not going to like that," said C.J.

"He'll get over it," I said.

"Wait a minute," said C.J. He walked over to a clump of weeds and kneeling down looked under the running board of a pickup. He pulled out a foot-long metal box.

"It's an ammo box." He opened it and looked inside. "Hell, I can use this. It's in good shape."

"Good. That'll make Felix happy."

We continued on toward the office as Felix was coming down the path to the driveway. He waved a slip of paper as we approached. "I got it," he said, handing the slip of paper to C.J. "The name I couldn't remember is Chezzy. Give him a call. Maybe he's still got it."

C.J. looked at the note. "Thanks a lot. You did good." He slipped it into a shirt pocket. "How much you want for this ammo box?"

Felix raised one eyebrow as he looked at it. "Where'd you find that?"

"Stashed under a pickup back there."

"What's in it?"

"Nothing. Look for yourself." C.J. raised the lid.

"I'll take fifteen for it. That good with you?"

"I got it," I said, and fished a twenty from my wallet.

Felix brought a roll of bills secured with a rubber band out of his pants pocket and started to make change.

"Naw. Keep it," I said. "You did good by us today."

"Thanks," Felix said. "If you need anything in future, give me a call. If I don't have it, I'll get on the computer and find it for you somewhere. Here's my card." He plucked a card from his shirt pocket with two fingers and handed it to me.

"Sure. Will do."

"There's something else I guess I better tell you all," he said.

"What's that?" C.J. asked.

"The wife just told me. Coincidence. Some guy was after that same car. He called here this morning asking about it."

"This morning?" I asked in disbelief.

"Yeah, she asked him how she was supposed to remember something that far back." He laughed. "Jeanette's never in a good mood mornings, and he called before we even opened up."

"Did she get a name?"

"No. She just told him that, hung up, and forgot about it until I came back in just now and started digging through the files."

"If he calls back again, get a name, will you?" I handed him a card with my cell phone on it.

He looked at the card. "St. Beatrice, Louisiana. What you doing all the way over here then?"

"Looking for that car," I said.

"I drove over there a couple of times. I got an aunt lives in Slidell."

"Say hello to her for me," I said, as we thanked him, got back in the car, and headed out to find Chezzy.

# 24

# CHEZZY RAINEY

A quick call to Chezzy Rainey confirmed he still had the Ventura. I felt a rush of relief up my spine and bit my tongue so I didn't call out *YES* and whoop and holler. I shot a look of victory over to C.J. as he drove back down the road toward the Interstate.

Chezzy fed me directions to his house that he described as halfway between Ocala and Brooksville. After a quick stop for gas, burgers and coffee, we made it to his house within the hour.

Chezzy was outside digging a border to a twenty-foot flower garden when we arrived. He jammed the shovel into the ground so that it stood upright like a pole, and came to greet us when we pulled up into his circular drive.

"Had any trouble finding me?" he asked. He pulled a red handkerchief from his pocket and wiped his sweating forehead, then twirled it and tied it around his neck. He had red hair fading to gray, and his face was red with exertion. He was a short but wiry and muscular man who looked like he worked out with more than just a shovel.

"Nope. You give good directions," I said out the window as C.J. parked the car.

We got out, shook hands all around, and then got right to it.

"You want to come on back and see the car?" Chezzy asked.

"Yes, we sure would," I said.

"Follow me then. It's over there behind that shed." He swung his arm and pointed toward the back yard. We followed him back around a yellow brick house, then past a spacious kennel where two coon dogs howled and scrambled with their front legs at the chain link.

"Quiet down!" Chezzy yelled at them. "Quit." They simmered down and dropped back from the chainlink onto all fours as we moved on toward a metal shed and then the prize we were looking for. The Ventura.

Chezzy started lifting off the grey canvas that covered it. C.J. and I stepped forward to help him fold it back and off the car. And there it was after all these years. No longer could its paint be called red though. It had faded to more of an orange in patches from the strong Florida sun, but the stream-line design was still intact. No dented fenders, no crumpled front end, no buckled windshield, such as we'd just been seeing at Fat Boy's.

"You bought this for parts?" I asked. "Looks like you could restore it."

"I've been giving that some thought. Block's cracked though. Needs a new engine. It would be a big investment, that's for sure."

"A little at a time. That's what I'm doing with my Mustang," I said. "I do what I can afford to do, then save up to do some more."

Chezzy wiped his face again with the back of his hand. "If I'm going to do it, I'd better get it moved into the garage for starters. Get it out of the weather."

"Would you consider selling it?" C.J. asked.

"Maybe. If the price is right."

C.J. looked at me and raised his eyebrows.

"So what would you call a right price then?" I asked.

"I hadn't really thought about it." He looked around, then leaned his head back and started tracking a chicken hawk that glided overhead.

"How about eight hundred? That work for you?" C.J. asked. I shot him a look. He smiled as he saw my surprise. "Now you all have me thinking about restoring a vintage car. What the hell. Why not? Takes me back to my high school days."

Chezzy closed one eye and ran his tongue over his teeth as he thought about it. He leaned his head one way and then the other as he stared at the Ventura. "There aren't many of them around any more. Let me think on it."

"Good deal. Think about it. But please don't let this car out of your sight in the meantime. It could be extremely important." I gave him my card.

Chezzy took it with one hand, squinted at it in the bright light, then snapped his fingers. "Louisiana, huh? What brings you all the way over here looking at old cars?"

"That's what the extremely important part is all about," I said.

C.J. fished his billfold out and flipped it open to the official looking I.D. that was hard to read in the strong sunlight. Chezzy squinted at it, then adjusted his visor hat to shield the sun even more. He placed a hand on the rear bumper of the Ventura, but jerked it back from the hot metal.

"This car isn't stolen?"

"No. Nothing like that. We can't go into any details right now. Just please don't let it out of your sight until you hear from us again."

"But what's the story on it? Now you have my curiosity up."

C.J. took a step forward. "Something happened a long time ago. Nothing to do with you, but this car may hold the answers to a cold-case crime over on the Gulf Coast."

"In Louisiana?"

"No. I'm from Bonita City," C.J. said. "He's from Louisiana." C.J. tilted his head toward me. "He's helping us solve a twenty year old crime."

"No shit? What? Kidnapping? Bank robbery?"

"None of the above," C.J. said. "But it's bad. And we really need you to keep this car safe."

"We talking murder here?" Chezzy lowered his voice.

The silence from both C.J. and I answered his question.

"Somebody got murdered in this car?" Chezzy's eyes opened wide, "but you can't talk about it right now?"

"No, no. relax. Nobody was murdered *in* the car," C.J. said.

"Hit and run then?"

"No. Not a hit and run."

"Okay, okay. I'll keep it safe. But when you call back, I want to know the details. Deal?"

"One day maybe," C.J. said. "And now, we better be getting back. Thank you very much for your time, Chezzy."

"Not a problem. Glad to help you all out."

We helped him roll the cover back over the sedan, then we all shook hands and C.J. and I left for Bonita City.

# 25

# TOO LATE

I was up early and ready to get going the next morning. I'd already showered and dressed and was ready to go out for breakfast, leaving Georgette still asleep.

I received the call just when I pulled into the parking lot of the restaurant. I didn't recognize the number on my cell phone.

"This is Chezzy Rainey. The guy with the Ventura? Good thing you left me your card," he said.

"What happened?" I felt the dread hit my stomach first, then creep up the back of my neck.

"Bad news. A guy came by here not too long after you left. He wanted to buy the Ventura also. I told him it wasn't for sale, and even if it was, somebody was ahead of him and had already made an offer. So he says, 'Then how come it's still sitting out there rusting away?' So I tell him that's not really his business, but I say it in a kind of nice way. So he offers me double whatever I got for it. I told him I couldn't do that. So he offers triple. I shake my head and tell him that's not how I roll. It wouldn't be fair to the other man who wants it. So he gives me a look that could kill, and leaves."

"Thanks, buddy. What a relief you didn't sell it to him. We need that car."

"Don't go thanking me yet. That ain't all."

"What? He came back again?"

"Somebody sure as hell did. The Ventura got torched last night. I wake up about two in the morning to the dogs barking like crazy out in their kennel, and when I go to see what's going on there's black smoke and flames out back. I ran for the hose and kept a steady stream on it, but it was too late to save it. It's a black mess right now. Good thing the gas tank was empty. So you can save the trip back up here."

"Did you report it?"

"Oh, yeah. I called 911 and reported it right away. Told them I had it under control with the hose and they didn't have to wake the Volunteer Fire Department we've got out here. But I wanted the time of it on record. I'll call the Sheriff soon as they open up."

"I'm really sorry to hear this. You don't know how sorry I am. And I thank you for calling right away. You're a good man. Don't touch the car. We will still want it. I'll get back with you on that."

"Trust me. You don't want it. Maybe I can get my Homeowner's to pay for what I have in it. Lots of luck with that, right?"

"Just don't touch it until you hear from me. Okay?"

"Okay, but the Fire Marshal will have to check this out. It's arson."

"When he shows up, ask him to call me, please. Tell him that car could be evidence in an old murder investigation and to please not touch anything in the driver's seat or area."

"All right. I will. Those seats weren't totally damaged. The oxygen must have gotten sucked out of the cab."

I took a deep breath of relief. "Glad you're a light sleeper."

"Always have been. Sometimes it pays."

"There any tracks in your yard that you can see?"

"No. I already looked. They must have parked out off the road somewhere a ways away and walked in."

"Not to tell you what to do, but can you walk along the road and see if you can spot any tracks where somebody might have pulled off the road?"

"Sure. I can do that."

"Do you remember what the guy was driving who wanted to buy it earlier?"

"Looked like one of those small new fuel economy cars. Maybe Japanese. Didn't pay that much attention. Don't like those new car designs much."

"Okay, Chezzy. Don't forget. Keep everybody away from it except the Fire Inspector and tell him to not touch…"

"The driver's seat and around there. I know the drill. I won't forget."

"It's very very important. Could be a case closer."

"I hear you."

"Thanks, Chezzy. We'll be in touch."

"Right."

We ended the call and I lost my appetite with that news so I continued on to the restaurant, and sat in a booth just wanting coffee to help me think.

A short stout waitress with Yolanda printed on a nametag pinned over a pink handkerchief folded like a flower came by holding a glass pot of coffee. She placed a mug on the table as though she read my mind.

"Just coffee, please," I said, motioning that she could hold off on the menu.

"You're not going to eat?" Her tone was motherly.

"Not just yet. Just had some bad news and I lost my appetite for now."

"Must be nice to lose your appetite. Wish I'd lose mine," she laughed, pouring the coffee. "Sorry you had bad news though." She put the plastic coated menu on the table anyway. "I'll leave this here for you just in case you get hungry again. Always a good idea to have something on your stomach when you're going through a hard time."

I nodded and she turned away toward another booth where a heavy set trucker wearing a Texas oil field equipment cap sat with his wife, partner on the road. Both of them were on their cell phones, probably to family members back home.

I pulled my own cell phone out and called C.J. reporting what Chezzy had told me.

"Holy shit, man," he said right off. "What the hell?"

"Yeah. How about that?"

"Not good. I know that much."

"It's bad all right. But it might be a good thing."

"How you figure?"

"It might be what we need to nail this guy. Can't tell yet."

"What's next then?"

"We have enough now to go to the Sheriff with this."

"Yeah. Sounds like it."

"They can take it from here. There's nothing more I can do, except keep my fingers crossed that they find something in that car."

"Right. You good to go? You want I should come with you?"

"No, I'm good. But thanks."

"If you need me, call me. I have to go in to the fire station tonight. But it's okay to call me if you need any help. I'm here for you, man."

"Thanks."

We clicked off, and I started drinking the coffee and watched absent mindedly as Yolanda brought plates of hash browns, eggs, sausage patties, and toast to the Texas trucking couple. They put down their phones and picked up their forks, both at the same time.

I signaled as Yolanda passed back by my booth.

"Change your mind?" she asked.

I nodded toward the Texans. "Bring me that same breakfast you just brought them, please."

"Told you," she smiled and hurried away.

# 26

# NEWS FROM HOME

By the time I returned to the cottages, Georgette was up and out of there, headed down the walkway wearing a shirt over her bikini ready to go for a dip in the pool. "Forget that," I said. "Something's come up. Come on back to the room and I'll tell you what happened."

"Sure," she said and when we were inside, she flopped on the bed. "What's going on?"

"I got a call from the guy that owns the Ventura. Somebody tried to buy it after we were there yesterday, and he said no. So, looks like whoever it was came back last night and torched it."

"What?" She sat up straight.

"Yeah. Torched it. Chezzy, that's the owner, called me just as I was going in for breakfast."

"This is bad," she said. She rubbed her arms like she was shivering. "I have goosebumps now."

"Yeah, well, no more waiting around for something to happen. It's time we talk to a detective at the Sheriff's Office."

She held up a hand. "I'm not going in there without a lawyer."

"Sure. Call somebody. Call that guy Jay you went to school with."

"I will. But it's Sunday. He won't be in the office. Can't it wait til Monday?"

"Hell no. They need to know about this right away. Call him at home."

She looked skeptical. "If it's torched already, what's the rush? I hate to call him on the weekend."

"Fine." I felt aggravated. "Then just call the Sheriff's Office without him."

"No way."

"Georgette." I put my hands on my hips and shook my head. "Get a grip. This is serious business. Call Jay."

"Oh, all *right*. Give me a minute. I have to call Mallory and get his number first."

"You do that. I'm going to grab a shower and shave."

I took a long hot shower, shaved, and by the time I came back out of the bathroom, she was headed back out the door.

"Where you going?"

"For my swim. Jay's out in the boat, his wife said. He won't be back for about an hour. And then the thing is, they have to hurry and get dressed for a wedding this afternoon, and after that they're going to the reception. She says it will be late by the time they get back."

"Did you tell her it's urgent?"

"Yes, more or less. I told her it's very important or I wouldn't have bothered him on the weekend."

"Dammit. I'm not sitting on this until Monday. First of all, that car has to be taken into custody. Who knows what will happen to it next? Second of all, I have business at home I have to take care of. I need to be there. We've been in Florida four days. The hell with waiting on Jay. I've got to turn this thing over to the Sheriff. Anything else would just be stupid....and irresponsible."

"But we don't really know anything," she protested. "And I'm not putting myself in their hands unless I have my lawyer by my side."

"Okay, then. I'll go talk to a detective myself. I'll tell him just enough to convince him to get that car picked up and locked up. I'll leave your name out of it and say my source is going to talk to him Monday when a lawyer can be present. Once I've turned it over to them, I can relax a little bit until Monday when you tell them what you know and we can get out of here. At least I'll know the Ventura is safe."

She squeezed her eyes shut and pressed her lips together.

"Well? What?" I asked. "Talk to me."

"I don't like it."

"Why not?"

"He'll make you tell him who I am."

"You really think I'm that stupid?"

"No. But he could probably guess it was your wife you were shielding."

"Now how's he going to do that? I'm going to call over there now and get this over with."

She headed for the door again. "Do what you want. You're going to anyway, no matter what I say." Her expression was bitter. "I'm going to the pool and work on my tan before they lock me up."

"They're not going to lock you up."

"So you say."

She threw open the door as though she planned to slam it, but as she crossed the threshold, she changed her mind, and instead, closed it softly behind her.

Once I dressed, I found a phone book in the bedside table, looked up the number for the Sheriff and called it. Being as how it was the weekend, there was a detective on call, and the dispatcher said she could put me through to him.

He didn't pick up right away and I sat on the edge of the bed waiting. Finally he answered, "Detective Olson."

"Detective, this is Edmond Mallet. I'm down here from Louisiana. I've got some information on a cold-case murder investigation that you will want to hear. I need to meet with you."

"How old a case are we talking about?"

"Twenty years."

"Can this wait until Monday then?"

"No. And there's a good reason for that."

"What's the reason?"

"I can't go into it over the phone, but I am an off duty police officer. So you can trust me, I wouldn't be bothering you with this if it wasn't urgent."

A pause. "All right. Can you come in to the Sheriff's Office? I'm at home but I can be there in less than an hour. Say forty-five minutes?"

"I'll be there."

I put the cell phone back into its holder and went out to the pool to tell Georgette the plan. She was applying suntan lotion to her legs and arms, rubbing it in vigorously, all her anger showing.

"I have to go. The detective is coming in to the Sheriff's Office to meet with me."

"Great. Have fun." She didn't look at me.

My phone rang. I pulled it out of the holder and clicked it open. "Uh-oh. It's Stubs," I said, and answered the call. "Stubs. What's going on?"

"You're not going to believe this," he said right away.

"What?"

"They found your stuff. Looks like all of it."

"The cops found our stuff?" I felt a rush of excitement. Georgette's head jerked up, eyes bright, her face no longer angry.

"No, the cops didn't find it. A kid did. That kid that does chores around your neighbor's farm. It was all dumped in Barney's woods. Just dumped back in the woods in a heap. Television set, stereo, radios, clothes, pots and pans. It's crazy."

"What the hell? Has it rained up there since we've been gone?"

"Nope. You're lucky. Everything's high and dry. Want me to go pick it all up and haul it back to the house?"

"Hell yeah. Damn, Stubs. I owe you big time. How'd you find out about this?"

"Barney couldn't find you at home so he called me. He didn't even know you were broken into."

"Call the Chief at home and tell him I said for you to go pick it all up. And look for tracks. You're a hunter. If you see any, mark them somehow. They must have driven a truck back in there. I'll get home as soon as I can, but right now there's something very important I have to take care of."

"So when will you get back here?"

"Soon as I can. I'm trying to get out of here now, but I can't just yet. I'll try to get back late tonight or tomorrow. You've got a spare key, just stow everything back in the house and lock up."

"Somebody's sure been messing with your head," Stubs said.

"No shit," I said. "Thanks, Stubs. I'll talk with you later."

I clicked the phone shut and turned to Georgette. "Okay, this changes everything. I've got to get back home. As soon as I talk to the detective I'm leaving. If you won't come with me now, then you'll have to stay here until you're done with the lawyer and the detective and then fly home."

"Without you? Are you kidding me?" Her eyes went wide in alarm.

"Why not? You'll be all right here. Ask Jay to pick you up Monday morning or take a cab to his office.

As soon as you're done here, get Mallory to drive you to the airport or take a cab. Fly in to Lafayette and I'll pick you up. What's so hard about that?"

"Stuck here without a car all day and tomorrow?"

"Why not? You can order some Chinese takeout, or walk to that little Mom & Pop's, or get another pizza. When I get back from the Sheriff's Office, I'll run you by the grocery store and you can pick up some things. There's a little fridge in the cottage. What's the big deal?"

"All right."

"All right what?"

"As in all right I'm coming with you. I'm not staying here alone while you're gone. Not after sending out letters to a possible killer."

I tried not to smile. "Great. Then hurry up and get dressed. We only have a little over half an hour before we have to be there."

"If the detective arrests me for withholding evidence, I'm getting a divorce. Just so you know," she said, getting up from the chaise and slipping on her sandals.

"Fair enough. But he's not going to. Cause you're going to wait in the car until I'm sure I can trust him, then I'll call you to come on inside."

# 27

# DETECTIVE OLSON

"So what is it you got that can't wait until Monday?" Detective Olson was tall, slim, and if I had to guess, I'd say he'd been in the Marines. He had sharp features, was clean shaven, his hair cut military style, and he looked like a man who expected to be saluted. He sat erect at his desk, and his expression said: *This better be good.*

"It all could wait until Monday, except for my fear that something else might happen to a car that may hold some damaging evidence concerning a murder in your county."

"I'm listening."

"Long story short, a previous owner of the car found out someone was possibly connecting him to a twenty year old murder, The Pitchfork Murder. Myron Miller."

There was a flicker of interest in his dark serious eyes, but his face quickly became expressionless again.

"I had located the car, a '79 Ventura, in a salvage yard near Ocala, then found it had been bought by a man living between Ocala and Brooksville. I went down there to see about it, and the owner, Chezzy, promised to hold on to it because I told him it could be important to a criminal investigation." I handed him the slip of paper with Chezzy's name and address on it.

"Then this morning, Chezzy called me to say someone had tried to buy it shortly after I left and he turned the man down. The man was angry that he couldn't buy it, but left. Then last night, the car was torched in Chezzy's back yard. He managed to put the fire out but the car is ruined." I paused to let this sink in for a minute, but I needn't have worried because Olson appeared unimpressed.

"So?"

"So, I'm hoping you will have the car picked up by the Sheriff over there in that county, so that it's safely in custody until your people can go over it for possibility of evidence from the Miller case."

"You suspect this car was somehow involved in Myron Miller's murder?"

"And I have a good reason. See, I am a Louisiana cop, but I'm on administrative leave. I had to shoot a man while on duty. I'd answered a 911 call, and the man shot at me after killing his wife. Because of this, I had the time off to drive my wife down to her twentieth class reunion here. I was bored, heard about the murder and started looking around.

"Because of a source, I found out some things, long hidden, that led me to suspect two possibilities.

The owner of that Ventura was one of the possibilities. My source and I sent letters to him and another man suggesting we knew about something they had done twenty years ago, but not revealing anything else. The letters asked for a meet at The Queen's Head Pub for Friday. The owner of the Ventura showed up. The other man did not. The Ventura man was angry about the letter, claiming it was a juvenile threat, and abruptly left. The other man may or may not have sent someone to take my source's photo, but somebody came into the Pub, took the picture, then hurried away out the back door." I waited to see how this went over, and watched Olson for any sign of interest, but couldn't read him.

"So I'm thinking the guy who showed up may be the one to follow up with, and if I could just find the car he drove back in high school, then it could be gone over for any evidence linking him to the murder."

"Which still leaves out why you suspected either one of the men in the first place," Olson said, his face carved in stone.

"I don't want to speak for my source. And my source is afraid to talk to you because of fear of arrest for withholding information in a homicide investigation. My source wanted to come here with a lawyer before telling the story."

Olson's eyes narrowed, and he remained very still. Finally, he spoke again. "So you want me to have this car picked up without knowing why I should, and why you are linking it to the Miller murder?"

"I do want you to do that, and it's okay with Chezzy. Just as soon as the Fire Marshal gets to his place to see it."

"Did the present owner of the car, this Chezzy, identify the man who came by after you left? Did you show him a picture of the man?"

"No. Didn't have one. But you can get one. He owns a business here in town."

"How can you say that? You have no positive ID on whoever it was."

"I'd put money on it though."

"This man you suspect. What's his name?"

"I want to leave that to my source to tell you, while telling you the back story."

"I'll need to hear the back story before I bother the Sheriff over there to go pick up a car for us. And there's nothing to convince me so far that the car was torched by this same man anyhow."

"I believe he's scared now that he's aware someone is onto him, and he's destroying any evidence that might implicate him in the Miller case. Why else would all this suddenly happen?"

"I still have to hear the back story first before even thinking about proceeding with any of this."

"Can you promise my source won't be arrested for withholding information all these years?"

"Depends on the story. And why this person didn't come forward at the time."

"Afraid. This person was a teenager and afraid to admit being anywhere near the crime scene."

Olson's eyes flicked to the left and to the right, then he jutted his chin and leaned his head back as he thought about all this. "Where is this person now?" His chair creaked as he sat up straight again.

"Here in town."

"Why is this person now willing to come forward after all these years?"

"I guess you could say I did a good job selling the idea."

"And you say you didn't know anybody down here and because you were bored at the reunion you started digging into all this?"

"Right."

"And so a complete stranger like you blows into town and gets somebody to reveal information from a notorious murder case that happened twenty years ago? You really expect me to believe that?" One side of his mouth lifted in amusement.

"I know how it sounds," I said, almost wishing we had just gotten into the car and gone back to Louisiana as soon as Stubs called.

"How long has your wife lived in Louisiana?" he asked.

"Long while. Many years."

"How long ago did she live around here?"

I paused. This guy was good. "Roughly twenty years," I finally said.

His dark eyes glittered like a hawk watching a rabbit as he picked up a pencil and rapped it a few times on the edge of the metal desk.

"So is your wife out in the car now?"

I didn't answer, just looked directly at him, hoping for the best.

"Bring her in then. Let's get this over with."

I waited, not sure where to go with this. "My wife?" I said, stalling for time.

"Come on, man. How thick do you think I am?"

I waited a few beats more.

"If she knows something or saw something, let's hear it."

"And you won't arrest her for withholding evidence?"

"Not unless she had something to do with the murder."

"No, of course not."

"Then bring her in. I want to hear what she has to say."

"Just so you know, this is all on me. Coming down here to talk to you. And now we're ready to pack up and drive back to Louisiana. I have a lot of urgent business to take care of at home. As soon as she's told you what she knows I want to leave with her. She came back down here with me in good faith because I talked her into going to the Law with this."

"Yeah, yeah. If she didn't do anything, you have no worries. Go get her."

# 28

# HELD OVER

While Olson listened to Georgette's story, I waited in the lobby, alternating between sitting on one of the row of chrome and black straight chairs and pacing up and down on the tile floor to the double glass doors and back. Up, down. Up, down. Being a Sunday, there was barely any traffic out on the street, and the lobby was quiet. A man sitting behind protective glass at the reception desk paid no attention to me and kept writing as I kept checking my watch, wondering how the minute hand could possibly move at such a snail's pace.

Olson kept her in there for almost half an hour, so it was a great relief when he finally came halfway down the hallway from his office, and beckoned to me. I walked down the hallway and he led me back into the office. Georgette looked grim, and her face was pale as she gripped the sides of her chair. She gave me no look of recognition, just stared ahead, lips pressed tightly together.

"Have a seat," Olson said, and he returned to his chair behind the desk.

"I know you said you wanted to take Georgette back to Louisiana right away, but I want her to stay here until tomorrow so my partner can interview her as well…with her lawyer if she wants."

"But, she's told you all she knows, hasn't she? And you still want her to stay here? We've got to get back."

"There's a lot to this story. If they'd known all this in the first place, the investigation would have been quite different. Not knowing any of these details, they wasted thousands of hours of man-power searching for leads, when they could have followed these leads from the very first day. This case was reopened and reviewed every year on the anniversary of Myron's murder for well over fif-teen years. It's still an open investigation to this day."

He turned his hawk eyes on Georgette, who had grown even paler. "So, the inconvenience to you all and your plans to get back to Louisiana are really not of much interest to me at this point. I want my partner to hear Georgette's story in person, and so she stays until he can do that tomorrow. We need to go through it all over again."

"And the Ventura?"

"We'll take it from here," he said, then turned to Georgette. "I want you to go back to The Cottages where you're staying and be back here tomorrow so we can go over all the details again with my partner. Understand?" He narrowed his eyes.

"Yes," she whispered.

"Bring your lawyer with you if you want," he said in an off hand way as though she didn't really have to bother with all that. He handed her his card and then gave one to me as well. "Call me as soon as you know what time your lawyer can come in with you."

She nodded, closing her eyes.

"And don't even think about going back to Louisiana with your husband until we go through this all over again. You with me?"

She nodded and clasped her hands together in her lap.

"If you don't do what I'm telling you, I will put a warrant out on you for withholding all this vital information in a murder case…for twenty years. You do understand that?"

"Yes."

"I can almost understand about the teenage fear and panic, but you haven't been a teenager for many years. You could have come forward long before now."

She nodded. "And I'm very sorry I didn't, Detective. It was cowardly, I admit it."

He didn't comment, just let her sit there feeling ashamed and miserable. Finally he pushed back his chair.

"All right. You can go now. That's all for today." He turned to me. "I'm glad you did the right thing and talked her into this. Now we just might have a chance at finally getting some justice for Myron's family. But from here on out, do not do anything further concerning this case. Do not speak to anyone about it. You should never have taken it into your own hands."

"Yeah, but we were able to bring you a strong lead even though we were interfering in your territory. You got to give us that."

"Another way of looking at what you did is, you may have spooked the killer, and he may be on the way to Mexico by now. And so far it looks like a real possibility he may have succeeded in destroying potential evidence by torching that car. You should have just brought your wife in to report to us before you got all creative with those letters you sent out."

"Have it your way. I'll stay out of it." I was angry and tried not to show it, but my voice betrayed me.

"And don't either of you speak to anyone about this. Except the lawyer you bring in on it. Right?" He did the hawk eye thing again. First at Georgette, then at me. "No one else knows about this, right?"

"Our friend C.J. He helped us at the pub and he went with me to hunt down the Ventura."

His face got darker. "C.J. who?"

"C.J. Jenks. You don't have to worry about him saying anything. He hasn't even told his wife."

"I know about Jenks. He organizes all the fundraisers for the Kids Burn Camp. We do security for him at the events. He's your friend?"

"Yes."

"Call Jenks then and tell him you've talked to me now and to continue to keep all this to himself. Very important."

"I will."

"Okay, both of you go on. We're done for now."

# 29

# TAKING OFF

By the time we got back to The Cottages, Georgette just wanted to go out and lie down in the sun by the pool. She started changing clothes, and I began pulling my clothes out of the closet and the bureau drawers in order to pack.

"What are you doing?"

"Getting ready to go, of course."

"You can't leave now."

"I have to leave now."

"But I have to stay over until tomorrow."

I stopped what I was doing and gave her my full attention. "We've been over this already. I have to get back and see about our things."

"Our things are in a heap on the floor wherever Stubs puts them. They're not going anywhere."

"Sure, and there's a nut case back home who is out of control. Who knows what he'll do next. You want me to wait until maybe he decides to burn down our house? And then there's the Mustang. Do you want me to wait until he comes around and burns the shed and the car to the ground? Somebody back home has put a target on my back. If you want to know the freaky things vengeful people will think up to do when they're worked up, ask any cop and he can tell you. You don't have to take my word for it."

"I can't believe you could leave me like this," she said, as she snapped the top of her bikini on. "Not after what we've just been through."

"Remember how your panties were placed under the wiper blades? It's just as well I'm going back and you're not. Who knows what he would try to do to you? That was a warning, whether you want to believe it or not. I've got a bad feeling about this and I want to get home. You'll be fine here. Before I leave, we'll swing by a store and pick you up some things. Tomorrow or the next day you can fly home whenever you are ready. End of story."

"Yes, and meanwhile I'm all alone and there might be a killer after me for all you know."

"Nobody knows you're staying here at The Cottages."

"You think. Nobody knew you were going to Ocala hunting for that car either."

"That could have been a coincidence."

"Coincidence my ass," she said. "How did he find you at Chezzy's then? More coincidence?"

"I'm not sure. Maybe he was coming to the salvage yard in person when he couldn't get an answer by calling on the phone, and he saw us there."

"And then maybe he followed you all back here and saw where we're staying."

"No. He was too busy trying to buy the Ventura. Nobody knows you're here except C.J. and the detective, but if you're so worried, I can take you to Mallory and C.J.'s to stay tonight. I'm sure they'd be happy to have you as their guest."

"No, my nerves are shot from all this. I don't want to see anybody right now. I just want to lie out in the sun and then come back to the room and watch a movie."

"That sounds good."

"You could leave me your pistol though at least."

"And how are you going to get on an airplane to fly home with it?"

She twisted her mouth and put her hands on her hips. "You know what? You're wrong to leave me at such a bad time. A husband is supposed to protect his wife. You care more about your Mustang and our things than you do me right now when I need you the most. Anyhow, this whole thing was your idea. I should have kept my mouth shut forever about Myron like I was planning to do in the first place."

"And would you admit that to Myron if his spirit was standing here in front of you right now?" I slung the suitcase on the bed and started folding clothes into it. "You cry about losing the stone out of the ring he gave you, but you would be okay with never helping to find his killer?"

"That was a rotten thing to say. You're cruel."

"No, I'm realistic. You're not. Get real."

"You know what? You're being so heartless, we might just as well get that divorce after all. Any man who would leave his wife under these circumstances doesn't deserve to be married anymore. Forget going to the store. I'll order out. Just go. I'm going to the pool. And don't think I'm flying back to Louisiana tomorrow. I'll stay right here and start looking for a job. I don't care if I have to work at Mickey D's. Or maybe I'll go be a mermaid at Weeki Wachee."

I zipped the suitcase closed. "Look, you're tired. You're upset. I'm going to forget you just said that. We can talk more when you're rested. Call me later on tonight when you're feeling better." I stepped forward to hold her, but she turned away and marched to the door. I watched her yank open the door so hard it slammed against the wall leaving a mark on the paint. She stopped abruptly on the threshold and turned around.

"While you're going through all those things that were stolen, please make a separate pile of my clothes and other belongings so you can box them until you can ship them once you have an address for me. You can keep the house. Just let me keep whatever we have left in the savings account so I can make a fresh start down here." She turned back around to leave, but stopped short again to call over her shoulder.

"Oh, and there is one more thing I almost forgot." She turned around again and smiled.

"Fuck you."

# 30

# GAME PLAN

I surprised myself with the attitude I had over this argument with Georgette. I was able to put it all aside on the drive home, deciding the whole business had freaked her out and she needed her space. I was willing to back off and give it to her without any anger on my part. I didn't know I was so easy to get along with. I also didn't pay a whole lot of attention to her ideas about divorce, but chalked it up to anxiety and a case of nerves over having to talk with Olson and his partner the next day. Once that interview with the detectives was over, she'd feel like a great weight was off her back and she would be herself once again.

Meanwhile, I had my own worries, and I placed my focus on what I would do once I got back home and how I would go about finding out who burglarized our house and who had it in for me. I had a good idea who it was and what I had to do was come up with a way of proving it. This was what I concentrated on all that long boring drive home across the Panhandle and on through Alabama, Mississippi, and Louisiana until I had crossed the twenty minute long Atchafalaya Swamp bridge and was near enough to home to smell and to feel the heavy humidity rising off the swamp waters and the bayous.

I was surprised to find the lights on and Stubs' GMC in the driveway. Hoss raced from the front porch to the car and threw his fifty pounds at me with the force of a linebacker. I hunkered down and hugged him tight. Georgette was one thing, but my dog was another, and Hoss was a thousand times happier to see me than my wife would be if she was around. But of course she wasn't around, and I was just as happy to see Hoss as he was to see me if that was even possible. It took me a good five minutes to calm him down enough to break away and go to the house. He leaped around me all the way up to the porch and through the front door.

As soon as we stepped inside, I could smell the cooking. Stubs had fixed a big pot of crawfish fettucini to welcome me home. When I entered the kitchen, he was holding a bottle of beer as he stood at the stove, stirring the pot.

"Hey, man," he said, all smiles. "You made it back." He lifted the bottle in greeting. "Grab you a beer out of the fridge. I bet you are starving for some good Cajun cooking after that long trip."

"Of course," I said, tossing my cap onto a mounted row of hooks on the wall near the back door where all the other visor caps hung.

"Georgette still out in the car?" he asked, still stirring.

"Nope. She stayed in Florida this trip," I said, grabbing a beer from the fridge.

"Huh? Why's that?" he looked at me, frowning in confusion.

"She's mad at me," I said, popping off the lid.

"What'd you'd do that's bad enough for her to stay down there?"

"It's a long story. Best left untold," I said. "She'll calm down. She's just upset, that's all. Not to worry."

"Okay, man. I stay out of married people business. Healthier that way. Look around. I put a lot of your things away best I could. Thought you'd be tired enough after that drive to have to come back to a heap of stuff just dumped in a pile in the living room." He nodded toward the cabinets and the drawers. "Pots, pans, knives in here." He jerked his head around toward the other side of the house. "TV, VCR, radios, stereo all that's back in the den. Hooked it all back up for you. Didn't think you'd be up for unsnarling all those wires when you're tired out and all."

"You are something else, Stubs," I said. "I owe you."

"Naw. That's what cousins are for. You'd do the same for me."

I walked toward the archway to the hall that led to the bedrooms and the den to see all the work Stubs had done putting things away. Hoss followed me along for the tour, padding along behind me as we circled the house. The den was back almost to where it had been. The bedrooms were back in shape and all was once again well at the Mallet house.

I breathed a sigh of relief and said a little prayer of thanks for having such a great cousin. The way I figured it, we were double cousins because our grandfathers on our fathers' side were brothers and they had married our grandmothers who they had met on a fishing trip near Houma. Our grandmothers were sisters, so we had a double dose of genes from that history. This explained a lot as to why we'd always gotten along so well ever since we'd been little kids. Of course it also could have worked the other way, and we could have been so alike we hated each other, but that was not the way it worked out with the both of us.

I got into police work and Stubs became a carpenter and also made cypress furniture in his shop at home. He was a craftsman and could make anything anybody wanted, including gun cabinets, so he had always done all right for himself between pick up carpentry jobs and his workshop furniture business on the side.

By the time Hoss and I returned to the kitchen, Stubs was serving up our plates. "Throw some forks on the table and we can eat," he said. I grabbed some mats and forks out of kitchen drawers and placed them on each end of the table. Since Georgette was gone, I tore us each a paper towel instead of a folded napkin as she would have done.

Stubs carefully set each plate down and pulled out a chair. "Let's eat," he said.

"You're one in a million," I said to him as I sat at my usual place and watched the steam rising from the heaping serving he'd given me. Hoss settled himself in his corner and watched us with eager eyes hoping we'd leave some for him.

Stubs said the blessing as was the regular practice of both our families whenever we sat down to a meal, and then we ate in silence for a while. I hadn't realized how hungry I was and had eaten half the plate before Stubs asked me, "So, what's the game plan?"

I looked up. "Game plan?"

"Yeah. Who do you think has got it in for you?"

"You mean who broke in here, stole all our stuff, and then dumped it off in the woods next door?"

"Yeah, that guy. Got any theories? I know I do." He raised the beer bottle and finished it off while keeping his eyes on me.

"I'm thinking it's maybe Gus. Leon's brother. He spread it around town that I better watch my back."

Stubs nodded. "That's what I'm thinking too. So how are you going to find out if it's him or not?"

"I thought about it all the way back here. What I have to do is get some evidence on him before he makes his next move. He's messing with me, so there will be more to come. I didn't even tell you all of it."

"What else did he do?"

"Left a pair of Georgette's panties on my windshield."

"Damn. That's heavy." He made a face. "Bet you had homicidal thoughts after that maneuver."

I nodded. "Worse than that."

"Right. Not only homicide but a little bit of torture thrown in for good measure. And he knew what that would do to you too. Son-of-a-bitch. Of course if it's Gus, he's always been a total bastard. Even as a kid. His father used to beat the crap out of him cause he was such a nasty kid, but it didn't do any good."

"Somebody spit in our spittoon in the living room. It sure as hell wasn't Georgette or me. We never used that spittoon. It's an antique just for show. I turned it over to Ira for lab work."

"So you want to get some DNA from Gus to see if it's a match up with the DNA in the spit? I know Gus chews. I've seen him enough times with a wad stuck in his lower lip."

"That's the plan. But going about it won't be easy. Gus is smart."

"There's got to be a way."

"Oh, there is. I just haven't thought of it yet."

"Have you seen him at all since the shooting?"

"No."

"I see him at Sparky's a lot. He stops there for gas. Usually buys a couple of cold ones in the afternoon and plays poker on the machines in the game room over there. He's addicted to those dopey video poker games. When I play it's gotta be with real people sitting around a table, me."

"That's a great idea, Stubs. If I can run into him somewhere like Sparky's, I can use that as an excuse to tell him how sorry I am about having to shoot his brother."

"That might get you laid flat out on the sidewalk with a broken nose and a tooth missing." He raised his upper lip and tapped at the gap between his teeth. "Take it from one who knows."

"Might. But maybe I'll get lucky and get him to talk to me long enough that he'll toss a can he's been drinking from into a trash can. Or maybe he'll spit some more tobacco juice on the sidewalk."

"And then what?"

"They call it a surreptitious collection. You got to get it in a public place though."

"Why?"

"I guess so you don't go breaking into somebody's house and stealing their coffee mugs or the cigarette butts out of their ash trays."

Stubs nodded. "Or their toothbrush maybe, huh?"

I went back to work on the crawfish. "You know, Stubs, you did a fine job on this fettucini, I couldn't have done better myself."

"Thanks, bro. Glad you like it. And about that syrup collecting whatever DNA sample? Better take something with you to put it in. I wouldn't want to have to collect somebody's tobacco juice without gloves on."

I laughed with my mouth full.

"Know what I mean, Vern?" He gave me a smile wide enough to show the missing tooth again, then rose to go to the fridge. "Want another beer long as I'm up?"

# 31

# GUS

Later than night, after Stubs had gone back to his trailer, I tried to call Georgette to see how she was doing, but she wouldn't pick up. I left a brief message that I hoped she was feeling better and that I'd gotten back to find everything put away in its place thanks to Stubs. I figured she was punishing me and that she probably wouldn't talk to me for another day or two until she calmed down, so I wasn't worried.

She had never cursed at me before and that was hard to get my mind around, but I just chalked it up to extreme anxiety over the whole situation down there on the Gulf Coast. Georgette tended to be high strung which had a lot to do with the headaches even without the guilt about her big secret. I liked to think that I was man enough to give her a pass over both cussing me out *and* wanting a divorce. And once she cooled off we would put it behind us and never refer to it again.

Hoss slowly worked his way up onto the bed as I was dozing off and I let him stay there at the foot of the bed. By morning however, he'd worked his way lengthwise so he was stretched out full length on his back, paws in the air. As soon as I got up he leaped off the bed and went to the door to be let out.

By the time I made coffee and sliced up some potatoes for the skillet, I had made my plans for the day. I needed to call my parents as I hadn't called them for over a week. They had retired to a house-boat over in Levee Town. They owned the house we were living in and Georgette and I had been renting to own all this time.

When the eggs, potatoes and sausage were ready, I ate, and then called them. My mother answered the phone and I told her as little as possible about what we'd been doing. "Georgette wanted to go back to Florida for her class reunion," was pretty much all I let her know.

"So come on over and tell us about your trip," she said.

"I can't right now. I've got a lot to catch up on over here."

"You all can take a break for an hour and run over to see us. Did you take pictures?"

"Should have."

"You went all the way down to Florida and didn't even take pictures?"

"Sorry, Ma. I didn't think of it."

"That's crazy."

"We were pretty busy."

"Was Georgette glad to go back after all these years? Is she glad to be back here now?"

"She didn't come back with me. She's staying down there for a while."

"What? You have got to be kidding. She didn't come back with you?"

My parents went everywhere together. My mother hardly ever goes anywhere without my father, except for her weekly *bourrée* game with her friends in the back room of Roy's Lounge in Leveetown or her Ladies' Altar Society meetings.

"She's got some things to do down there," I said, being as vague as I could.

"You're not telling me something. I can always tell. What's wrong?"

"Nothing's wrong." Once my mother catches a scent she is on it like a coon hound with his nose to the ground.

"Yes, there is. I can tell by your voice."

"Okay, we had an argument, that's all. She's staying down there until she cools off."

"I never heard of such a thing. That's what you get. Why, oh why, didn't you marry a Cajun woman, son? Your life would have been so much easier with someone who knows how we do things around here."

"I know plenty of Cajuns who aren't that easy to get along with."

"That's not the point. Her gumbo is watery and she can't make a good cup of coffee to this day. I've tried and tried to help her."

"Mom, not everybody gets up before dawn and grinds their own coffee beans like you do."

"And she buys Folger's. *Folger's. Ohhh, mais là.*"

"So buy her some Community for Christmas. Enough. Leave it alone, okay?"

"All right. For now. But you get over here and see us, you hear me?"

"I will soon as I get caught up with all I have to do."

"Give me some notice and I'll make stuffed peppers with crawfish and crab meat. Your favorite."

"I'll definitely give you notice for that, Mom."

"And your father will probably have some fresh fish on the grill to go along with it."

"I'll get over there soon as I can."

"You'd better."

After we said our goodbyes, I cleaned up the kitchen, and went outside to throw some balls for Hoss. I had to mow the grass. I had to go by the neighbor's and tell him how grateful I was to get our stuff back from his woods. I had to stock up on groceries and check in with the Chief about the return of the stolen goods. And I had to keep my eye out for Gus so I could proceed with the plan.

I had a busy day ahead of me, and it was a nice day for it. The clouds were puffy and sparkling white. The sky was a clear blue and looked like a Disney movie, and the air was less humid than it had been the night before. When I'd thrown the ball enough for Hoss so that he got tired of it and quit bringing it to me, I went back to the house to drink another cup of coffee and to get the keys for the shed where I kept the rider mower.

# 32

# HO-HO

"You were right about that deer camera, Edmond," said Chief Ira, leaning back in his office chair.

"You found one?"

"We found two. One in back and one in front of Skinny's trailer. And guess who was on the one in back?"

"Tell me."

"Horace Duchamps, Junior," he said with a small smile.

"Ho-Ho was at Skinny Dupuis' trailer? The night he drowned?"

"Better than that, he went inside the trailer, and then came back out with Skinny about half an hour later. And that's the last anyone saw of Skinny that night that we know of."

I whistled. "That's a slam dunk, huh, Chief?"

"Circumstantial as hell, but no slam dunk. We'll have to see what he has to say first."

"What are you waiting for?"

"Haven't found him yet. Horace Sr. says he's gone fishing somewhere in the Basin and he hasn't seen him for a while."

"That's not good. He'll tip him off you're looking for him and he'll take off for Texas or even further down the road than that."

"I know it."

"His father's rooster fights get busted up and the word is Skinny is the snitch, and all of a sudden Ho-Ho goes by his place to visit. Looks bad."

"We'll find him."

"No doubt about that," I said. "I came by to tell you everything my cousin Stubs picked up in the woods seems to be all of what the thief took."

"That right?"

"Seems to be all there."

"So the whole burglary was some kind of a message."

"Yep. Somebody paying me back for something I did, and I suspect it's Gus Vidrine.".

The Chief nodded. "Could be."

"There was more too, Chief." I told him about the panties on the windshield.

He shook his head. "Whoever would do a thing like that concerning a man's wife hates your guts, son. Be careful."

"It's true. And whoever did it is trying to warn me that they're not above hurting her as well as me."

"Watch out, Edmond. Keep Georgette close."

"She's down in Florida still. He can't hurt her down there. And just in case I can get a match up from the lab work on the spittoon, I'm going to try to get a DNA sample from Gus."

"And how do you plan on doing that?"

"I'm going to try to talk to him about how sorry I am that I had to shoot Leon, and hope I can catch him with a beer can that he tosses in the trash can at Sparky's. He goes by there a lot I hear. Plays video poker in the back game room."

Ira took a deep breath, crossed his arms in back of his head and rocked back in the chair. "Sounds like a plan, son. Go for it. But remember, you're not on duty. Don't get carried away and cause any problems. I want this investigation on you to be over with and no delays cause I need you back on duty. We're short handed around here."

# 33

# BAYOU CHIEN

While I was at the grocery store, I picked up two cases of Bud for Stubs and took them by the trailer. His place was on a dirt road across the Bayou from St. Beatrice. As the crow flies, only five minutes from our house, but to get there I had to drive up the Bayou five miles to an old concrete bridge and then through some winding back country roads with fields and deep ditches on both sides into an isolated community known locally as *Bayou Chien*.

The beagles were howling back in their kennel and his rat terriers bolted around the trailer to greet me. I went around the trailer to his workshop in the back where between the Cajun radio station KOUI and the screaming of the grinder, he hadn't heard the barking. He looked up, safety goggles in place, and then immediately shut off the grinder.

"Hey, come on in," he said, reaching up to the shelf over the workbench to turn down the volume on the radio.

"Brought you some brews as thanks. It's not enough for all you did, but it's a start."

"That's great. But you didn't have to do anything, bro. I was just glad to get your stuff back safe under your roof again."

I stacked the cases by the door. "You did more than anyone else would have done. But, I got some ice cream in the truck so I got to get back to the house. Just wanted to bring these by and tell you something to look out for."

"What you got?" He wiped his face with a shop rag.

"The Chief is looking for Ho-Ho. I can't tell you why, but if you hear anything let me know, will you? Or tell the Chief."

"He can't find him at the Duchamp place?"

"His daddy says he's gone fishing in the Basin. I don't believe it."

"I'll keep an eye out. I did hear a rumor that they moved the rooster fights to a new location."

"Already?"

"Wherever it is, it won't be easy to find. Probably where Ho-Ho is at right now helping his old man build a new arena."

I nodded. "Thanks, Stubs. I'll pass it on to the Chief. Give me a call. Got to go."

"See you later, man. Take it easy. And watch yourself. Keep Hoss inside when you're not home. You know how nasty people think nothing of poisoning an enemy's dog."

"Way ahead of you on that, Stubs. Left him in the house while I was out. Thanks."

"Thanks for the beers. Come back and have a couple with me when you get lonesome over there with Georgette gone and all."

"I will, but I don't have time to get lonesome right now. Too much going on around here."

"There's no rest for the wicked," he said, wagging a finger at me.

"That's a fact," I said and headed back for the truck.

# 34

# STUBS REPORTS

When I got home, I called Georgette again but she still wouldn't pick up. I left a brief message asking her to at least let me know she was all right. I had no sooner put away the groceries when Stubs drove up in his GMC.

He came around to the back kitchen door and I called for him to come on in as I jammed a few pizzas into the freezer.

"What's going on?" I asked as he leaned against the counter, and I stacked cans of chili and pork and beans on a shelf.

"So, I'm passing the hardware store and there's Billy LeBlanc loading rolls of chicken wire into his Ford 150."

"Yeah, so?"

"Billy's a good buddy of Ho-Ho's. So, I'm right away suspicious."

"Why? He lives in the country. Probably raises chickens, him too."

"It's more than that. He's got two big bags of other hardware. So I'm wondering if they're not fixing to build a portable arena for the rooster fights. That way they can pick up and move when things get too hot."

I hung a net bag of red potatoes on a nail so the air could get to it. "Maybe. Could be. I wouldn't necessarily jump to that conclusion, me."

"Yeah, well I did. I know those guys better than you do and I don't trust either one of them. So I turned off at the next corner, and when he drove off from the parking lot I hung back and followed him down the road all the way out of town."

"I know enough about those guys to know they don't trust anybody at all, not even their own grandmother. So how did you figure you could follow one of them out of town?"

"Are you forgetting I used to run moonshine for Paw-Paw starting at age thirteen? I know every back road and dirt road and shortcut in six Parishes. No way he was going to spot me. I stayed back roughly a quarter mile until we had gone about twenty miles and I saw what I could have predicted at the beginning of the run."

I threw a package of sausages into the fridge. "He ducked into the woods somewhere?"

"Right on," Stubs said with a look of triumph. "And I'm pretty sure those woods belong to Gervis LeBlanc."

"That old man?" I shifted some beer bottles in the fridge to make room for a carton of O.J.

"That old man is one of Billy's six or seven uncles on his father's side."

"So he was taking the chicken wire to his uncle's place?"

"Not really. Gervis doesn't stay out there. He lives in his house in town. He keeps all those acres of woods just for hunting."

I wadded up the empty plastic bags and stuffed them into a container we keep for the purpose. "So maybe......."

"Right. That's maybe where Ho-Ho is holed up. That's maybe where they're getting ready to set up the next round of rooster fights. Gervis either likes the idea or he doesn't even know about it."

I nodded. "Stubs. You're all right. We need to go out there at night and see if any lights are visible from the road."

"When? When you got in mind to go?"

"I'm not exactly tied down these days. How about tonight? If it looks like there's somebody staying back in those woods, I'll let the Chief know. He can alert Sheriff Quebedeaux himself. I'm not supposed to get involved in anything right now."

"Tonight's good. I'll pick you up. What time?"

"Whatever you want. Around nine. Those boys might go to bed early and shut off the lights."

"Those two? Go to bed early? You got to be kidding. How about we go out there after ten. That work for you?"

"I'll be waiting."

# 35

# SATAN

At ten that night, Stubs' headlights arced through the front windows and I didn't wait for him to get out of the truck, just quickly flicked on the front porch light, let myself out the front door, locked up, and joined him.

"You ready to find Ho-Ho?" he asked as I slid onto the seat.

"Ready."

"The man with the plan," he said, as he kicked up some gravel backing out of the driveway that pinged beneath the truck. He scratched off down the blacktop showing off like a teenager.

Stubs' radio was tuned to the Cajun station, KOUI, and because they often played country, Gene Watson was singing *Together Again*. Stubs shot me a sideways glance.

"You missing Georgette yet?"

"Haven't had the time to miss her. It's been non-stop since I got home."

"Yeah, right," he smiled.

"It's true."

"You talk to her yet?"

"Is this an interrogation?"

"Okay, I'll butt out. Sorry."

"It's gonna be okay, Stubs. She'll get over it."

"Sure," he said, turning off onto the main road that would lead us west toward Eustis, the St. Beatrice Parish seat, and beyond to a long stretch of farms and woods going on for miles with only an occasional crossroads town to break it up.

"What's our strategy?" I asked.

"We park on the road like we're making a piss stop and we stare deep into those woods looking for any lights. Flickering lights, dim lights, whatever. There's probably no electricity out there, but maybe they have a generator. Who the hell knows?"

"Kerosene lanterns. Coleman lanterns."

"Whatever. If there are lights out there, then we go in and look to see if Ho-Ho is lurking anywhere around the place."

"I can't go into those woods though. The Chief told me to stay away from any involvement in any kind of action around here. Long as I'm on suspension, I got to listen to the Chief."

"Edmond, just when did you turn pussy on me?"

"Stubs…it's my whole career on the line. I'm still being investigated, remember?"

"Nobody's going to catch you. We're going in Ninja style."

"If Ho-Ho is in there somewhere and he hears a twig snap, he'll come looking for us with a shotgun."

"But we won't make a sound. We be like ghostly Ninjas, us."

"I can't take the chance."

"Oh, so the Chief put out a BOLO on Ho-Ho, but you don't plan on letting him know where Ho-Ho is, cause we can't locate him for sure, cause you're too nervous? Is that the way it is? Hell, I have to go in there on my own, I guess."

I let the conversation hang there and watched oncoming headlights for a few miles. Johnnie Allen was singing, *Light in Your Window* as I weighed the pros and cons of seeing this adventure through without getting hammered for it.

By the time Stubs slowed and pulled off onto the shoulder of the road in the middle of a long stretch of black trees, I'd made up my mind. He turned off the radio as he let the engine idle.

"You see anything over there through that blackness?"

We both kept our eyes searching back and forth, back and forth. "Let me pull up a little further." He drove the truck back onto the road and moved ahead another quarter mile. "Now?" He pulled off the road again and we scanned the area still straining our eyes. This time we saw a dim light set back deep into the woods.

I looked at him and he nodded. "That's gotta be them. Let's go." He raised the cover of the console and pulled out two headlamps, handing me one. "Here you go."

I adjusted the lamp onto my head, centered it, tightened the band, and got out of the truck. He took two small cans of pepper spray out of the console. "Here," he tossed me one. "In case they've got a guard dog roaming around. Stick this in your pocket."

"You sure come prepared."

"Just call me the Midnight Creeper," he said, turning on his headlamp. "We'll just use my light for now," he said. "Follow me."

We made our way slowly through the woods, stooping under vines, watching for deadfalls, and placing our feet with care. As we moved closer to the light, we began to be able to make out the outlines of a metal building about eight hundred feet back from the road. By then, we were close enough to hear someone laughing.

As we approached the building, Stubs pointed toward the left side where a pool of light spilled out into the darkness. He clicked off his headlamp and I followed him to the corner of the building where we hunkered down, moving awkwardly on bent knees toward the window. Barely raising the tops of our heads to eye level at the base of the window, we could see some of the interior of the corrugated metal thirty-foot long shed. The light was coming from two green Coleman lanterns hanging from hooks suspended from the ceiling on wires.

One man was exercising a red rooster by lifting him up high and then flinging him toward a table so he had to flap his wings hard to make a landing, skidding onto the metal surface. The rooster was tied to a string so the trainer could snatch him back up again and again, repeating the exercise. A column of caged roosters was stacked against the wall.

Ho-Ho was there all right. He was helping Billy attach hinges to panels of chicken wire lying side by side on the floor. He wore bib overalls with no shirt underneath so fresh bright tattoos of a fighting pit bull and a skull with a red rose were visible on his dark arms, tattoos so fresh that they glowed with the Vaseline smeared on to protect them as they healed from recent needle work. A bottle of Black Jack stood half empty beside them next to a pile of crushed beer cans and the stubs of hand-rolled cigarettes.

I poked Stubs with my elbow and jerked my head toward the road. "Let's go," I mouthed. I turned away from the window and started to return to the truck with Stubs following. We moved just as carefully as before on our return trip, but when we were halfway back to the truck, the door of the building opened and a black pit bull bolted outside.

"Move," I said.

The dog immediately raised his leg by a tree, but it only took a minute for him to smell strangers on the property and he took off, crashing through the brush, leaves and vines on a direct path toward us.

"Run. Run like hell," I said, and we did. I flicked on my headlamp so we had even more chance of getting back to the truck without tripping on vines, and we just about made it. But then, within ten feet of the truck, the fifty-pound pit was on me. He snatched at the back of my jeans, clamping down on the wallet in my back pocket. I fumbled the pepper spray loose from my pocket, twisting to spray him in the eyes as I felt his teeth break through to the skin.

"I got this," Stubs yelled. He lunged for the dog's rear end, grabbing at him, and yanked with such ferocity, the dog let go, yelped once, and went down flat on the ground.

"What the hell did you do?" I asked.

"Just get the hell in the truck," he gasped.

We made it into the truck, just as someone started calling, "Satan. *Satan.* Here boy."

Stubs turned the key, and with a quick look in the rear view mirror, he roared off and got us the hell out of there.

"What did you do to that dog back there?" I asked, once we were safely a mile down the road.

"Twisted and yanked his balls as hard as I could. You ever try to open a pit bull's mouth when he's got his teeth into somebody? Can't be done." He wiped his hand back and forth on his jeans. "You got to go at it from the other end."

"Jesus, Stubs. Thank you. You saved my ass. Literally." Where the dog had torn my jeans was numb, so I didn't know yet how much damage he'd done. I twisted my body so that side was partially off the seat and up against the door.

"The dog's lucky I didn't yank his nuts off completely. I know one guy who had to do that, and he finished the job." Stubs wiped his forehead with the back of his hand. "Now call the Chief and tell him where he can find Ho-Ho and we'll call it a night. Just tell him you got a hot tip. You don't have to go into any of the details."

"You got that right," I said as I reached into the glove compartment where Stubs always keeps a pint of his own home brew in a mason jar. This batch had a half peach floating in it. I took it out, unscrewed the lid and gulped half of it. It burned all the way down, but I needed that to take my mind off the dog bite.

"Thanks, Stubs," I said, and handed the jar to him.

"Don't mind if I do," he said, as he took the jar and finished it off.

# 36

# GUS

Satan had broken the skin in two places despite the protection of the wallet, and I knew I couldn't go to a doctor with it because doctors are required to report dog bites. They would demand to know where the dog was that bit me, and being arrested for Trespass was going to jeopardize the investigation currently involving me, and it didn't matter that I was helping local Law Enforcement with a BOLO. No. A doctor was out of the question.

Satan was wearing tags on his three-inch wide leather collar, so I was pretty sure he was up to date on his rabies shot. I soaked in a hot tub with Epsom salts and then applied the good-for-everything Neosporin we always keep in the medicine chest. A few beers, a late monster movie, and I fell asleep on the couch in the TV room.

The next day I was stiff all over, and the bruise around the tooth marks had developed into an ugly stain on my rear end that would soon bloom into as bright colors as Ho-Ho's freshly tattooed red rose. My head felt like it was in a vise, but I was not in a lousy mood. I was glad we'd accomplished what we had, and that I had a can-do cousin as great as Stubs watching my back. It's not everybody that can say that, not by a long shot.

I swallowed some aspirin and brewed extra strong coffee with a towel wrapped around me, fed Hoss, and carried out my usual morning routine, trying to get ready to go find Gus. I had to figure out a way to capture something he had either been smoking or been drinking from. I planned to make as many passes by Sparky's that I needed to until I saw his glossy black, chrome-railed Chevy in the parking lot.

I wanted to avoid seeing the Chief as long as possible. I didn't want him asking questions about how I'd gotten tipped off about Ho-Ho. The Chief knows me well and I might look like I was hiding something. Yet if I could get something that had Gus's DNA on it, I had to go by the station with it anyway. The more time that went by before I had to face Ira, the better, and the less likely it would be that he would notice I was being secretive.

Sparky's was run by a man from Pakistan. He hired all women workers to run the place, and he seldom showed up. I went by there and filled up my gas tank. No Gus. I went through the car wash and did some errands, then passed by there again. Still no sign of him. A few more hours and a few more passes in between trips to the lumber yard, the hardware store, and the feed store and still no Gus.

I stopped off at Miss Josie's and bought a takeout of the day's specialty, shrimp *étouffee*, drove to the public boat ramp on the bayou and ate it standing up with a plastic fork and leaning against the tailgate while I watched a fisherman pull his boat out of the water, sliding it onto his trailer.

Some baby ducks floated in a row near the opposite bank and I hoped they'd make it to adulthood. They might if no alligators came patrolling through the area. We didn't get many, but they did show up from time to time. The fisherman secured his boat and got back into his pickup to drive back up the sloping bank to the road. I tossed the takeout box into the public trashcan and got back into the truck to go make another pass at Sparky's.

It hurt to sit, so I leaned one way as far as I could, keeping my weight off the dog bite. It was awkward, but you do what you have to do in order to keep moving. This fifth time nailed it, and sure enough, there was Gus's fancy Chevy. It even had chrome running boards. Gus had gone through a large settlement from a car accident like a hot knife through butter. Between the casino, the racetrack, off-track betting, and fancy toys like that Chevy, he had chewed his way through all the big insurance payout within a few years.

I parked my truck and went on inside, nodding to a few people who were coming out, and looking around the store for any sign of Gus. The video poker machines were set along a side wall and hidden by pressboard panels so people could do their betting in private. I walked back to the door

of the makeshift little gambling room and opened
the door a crack. Gus was busy at a poker machine,
his back to me, a Corona by his side set on an odd
shaped triangular side table. No one was playing the
other two machines. I closed the door and crossed
to the refrigerated units along the front wall, found
a cold bottle of Corona, and went to the counter to
pay the cashier.

I then walked back through an aisle of canned
goods and bags of chips toward the video poker
room while removing the bottle cap. I slipped inside
the door and moved toward Gus. He was murmur-
ing and grunting and so focused on the game he
was playing, I was able to switch beers with him before he even knew I was behind him. I backed out of
there just as he won and the machine started pump-
ing out quarters. He was laughing at his good luck
and congratulating himself out loud as I passed on
through the store toward the double glass entrance
doors, Gus's Corona held tightly at its base in my hot
hand. Now I had to get this over to Chief Ira ASAP.

# 37

# GEORGETTE

Renée told me to have a seat because the Chief would be back in a few minutes. So, being as how I wanted to hand the Corona directly to him, to keep contamination at a minimum, I sat on a metal folding chair and waited. I was reviewing in my mind what I would say to him if he asked me where I got the tip about Ho-Ho's whereabouts, when my cell phone rang.

Finally Georgette was breaking her silence. "About time," I said, as I answered the call and walked outside the building so Renée couldn't hear what was sure to be an explosive conversation.

"I know, I'm sorry not to call. I stayed mad for a while. I'm sort of over it now though...I think."

"Okay, you're sort of not mad," I said. "So what else is going on? How did it go with the interview?"

"It was intense. They went at me from every direction. It's a good thing I had Jay with me. I was a wreck by the time he drove me back to the cottage."

"That was the end of it?"

"So far. Haven't heard another thing from them. They said I could go, and that's when we finally left. We were there for two hours. Two grueling hours that felt like four. They gave me coffee to keep me going. I've never been so glad to get out of a place as I was that drab little icy cold interview room. Icy cold, but it was hell."

"You can't blame them. They might have solved the case years ago if you'd told them what was going on that night. Anyhow, it's over. So now what?"

"I paid the desk clerk for a week's stay here at The Cottages. It's much cheaper by the week." Her voice dropped to not much above a whisper. "I was feeling safe here, but now I'm scared."

"Why?"

"C.J. just called me. They picked up Eric Snyder."

"That's fast work."

"Not so fast. He's out already."

"Say what?"

"You heard me. He bonded out. Twenty-five thousand dollar bond was the highest the judge could go on the torched car. Aggravated destruction of property or something like that. He's out and I'm scared."

"He doesn't know where you're staying."

"Maybe he is going to make it his business to find out."

"So fly home. What's stopping you?"

"I'm thinking about it. But I'm already paid for another week, and I have a party to go to Saturday."

"A party?"

"Some kind of pool party. An old friend and his wife are throwing it at their house. Don't remember if you met them or not. The Flahertys?"

"Don't remember the name. How'd they find you?"

"Mallory. She gave them my number. It'll be fun. They've even hired a live band."

"So when did they invite you to this pool party?"

"Just yesterday."

"So you're scared, but you won't be flying home cause of a party?"

There was a pause as though she was waiting for me to say more. I didn't. Finally she said, "I don't think I'm ready to come back to Louisiana yet. I might just go buy a pistol instead to keep on my bedside table. What do you recommend I get?"

"I don't recommend you do anything but fly home. But if you insist on being a hardhead and staying down there, then go find yourself a .22 or a .38. Either one will do the job. If he comes at you, go for the chest. That way if your aim is off, it will hit somewhere vital and stop the attacker."

"Most men would want to come right back down here and protect their wife who is probably in a lot of danger."

"I'm not most men, and anyway most men don't have a wife who wouldn't have gotten on an airplane by now to fly home." I was pacing back and forth in front of the Police Station by this time. "But of course I realize that even though you're scared, a pool party is too good of a deal to pass up."

"See? Now you're mad. I'm scared and you just get mad. Sorry I called at all." She clicked off and I was so angry I made a fist and almost punched the brick wall. I restrained myself just in time to avoid the pain of skinning and bruising my knuckles. It wasn't worth it. I had enough discomfort with the dog bite and was fresh out of physical tolerance.

Renée came to the door just then and beckoned me back inside. "The Chief's just come in the back way," she said. "Come on in. He wants to talk to you." She glanced at my hand, still formed into a fist. "Having a bad day, are we?" she asked.

# 38

# GEORGETTE'S FEAR

After Chief Ira had stowed the Corona in a sealed plastic bag and labeled it to send off to Sheriff Quebedeaux in Eustis, he pointed to the chair in front of his desk. "Sit. The Sheriff made sure that stretch of road was watched for whenever Ho-Ho came out of there. The deputy saw a pickup coming out of there early this morning. Only he waited until they were way down the road so Ho-Ho wouldn't suspect his new location has been spotted. The deputy saw they weren't wearing seat belts and stopped the truck."

"Nice."

"After they brought Ho-Ho in on that BOLO for questioning, Mitch Lanclos interviewed him, but then Mitch had to cut him loose. Ho-Ho spun a story about how he and Skinny were just out walking the night he drowned and he has no idea what happened after they split up. Ho-Ho went home to bed and far as he knew that's where Skinny was headed. Home to bed."

"Can't get him on circumstantial?"

"No way. The prosecutor would never bring a case he can't win."

"At the very least, Ho-Ho shoved him into the bayou for ratting out the rooster fights."

"Sure he did. Can't prove it though. But don't worry. My daddy always told me, 'If a catfish didn't open his mouth, he wouldn't get caught'. Ho-Ho will get drunk and run his mouth. Just a matter of time. Probably before the year is out too."

I nodded.

"Interesting that you got that tip about his where-abouts. Who'd you hear it from?"

I shifted in my chair and cleared my throat, then muttered something about a man at a hardware store.

The Chief held up a hand. "Stop. Don't want to hear any more. Long as you weren't out there tracking Ho-Ho down while this investigation on you is still going on." He smiled. "Course I know you would never break the rules like that. Right?" He rolled his chair back. "Okay, that's it for now. I've got to write a report for the town meeting to-night. Keep in touch."

I nodded, got up and headed for the office door.

"And this time, please just stay home and lay low. You think?" he said.

I looked over my shoulder but he had already opened a file folder and was shuffling through some papers.

\* \* \*

When I got home, I fished out the card Detective Olson gave me and called him.

"Detective," I said, "You remember me? Edmond Mallet from Louisiana?"

"Sure I do."

"I just heard Eric Snyder bailed out. I'm worried for my wife. Georgette is still down there in Bonita City."

"You can relax. They just picked Snyder up again. The Judge ordered him to stay in the jurisdiction and he was headed up the Interstate with a car full of luggage."

"How'd you find out so fast?"

"The budget wouldn't allow for twenty-four hour surveillance once he went back home, but we have our ways to see somebody is keeping an eye on who-ever we need watched."

"Very glad to hear this. I'll tell my wife. Georgette will be relieved."

"Surprised she'd want to stay down here after all this."

"Yeah, me too."

"Now that Snyder's proved to be a flight risk, he won't be getting out anytime soon."

"Thanks. Good to know. Nothing yet on the Ventura?"

"Nothing yet. Takes time. But you know that."

"Yes."

"When you come back down, come on in. We'll talk."

"I will. Thank you."

"Okay then, later," he said and clicked off.

I right away dialed Georgette to tell her the good news. She didn't answer so I left a message about it, ending with, "He's not getting out this time, so you can relax and enjoy your extended vacation down there in La-La Land."

I knew I sounded resentful, petty, angry, etc., but a saint I am not, and I was angry with her for being obstinate, hardheaded, and enjoying herself so much without me. What got to me most of all was her not seeming to care whether she saw me again or not. They say anger always covers up hurt, and I had to admit it to myself. If I dug deep enough under the anger, there was hurt deep down in the mix.

Okay, I chided myself, enough of that. Either go back down there and have it out with her, or shut up and go fix up the shed like you started to do before all this Florida episode ever began. Get your mind off Georgette and her problems and go work on your own projects. Let her deal with her guilt and her boyfriend's twenty-year-old slaughter down there on her own. I had done what I could.

So I set up the sawhorses, plugged in the circular saw on an outside outlet and got to work measuring and cutting cypress boards to tighten up the shed. By the end of the day I had replaced a few damaged boards, replaced a few rusted corrugated metal strips on the roof, and tightened the place up so it would stay high and dry despite any heavy Louisiana rains.

The best thing I can do if I'm angry is to work it off and funnel that energy into hard labor, and that's what I had done by the end of the day. I was hot, tired, and no longer angry. I put a pizza in the oven and took a hot shower, then ate, and stretched out on the couch in the TV room to watch movies until I fell asleep. With Hoss in his bed lightly snoring and a Van Cleef Western I'd already seen three times, it wasn't long before I was asleep with the TV still on.

# 39

# A CONFESSION

C.J. called me next morning. "Hey, man. Did you hear?"

"Yeah, I heard. Eric's back in jail."

"That's old news. What's new is his confession. One of my buddies works in the jail. Eric confessed to being scared that he was going to prison for what he'd done. He was headed to Mexico when they picked him up because he was guilty as hell. But not for what you think. He was scared because of a hit and run when he was a teenager.

He ran into a homeless man walking by the side of the road one night. He'd been drinking and he panicked and left the scene. He thought that's what the letter you all sent him was all about. Is that crazy or what?"

"Bad for Eric."

"He's in deep shit even after all these years."

"That's really something. We spooked him with the letter and he freaks out over something else altogether. What are the odds?"

"I know. It's really wild."

"I talked to Detective Olson yesterday. Still no word back on the Ventura."

"You coming back down here to drive Georgette back home?"

"I don't know. She wants to be alone or something."

"We'll be seeing her Saturday at this birthday party coming up. Our old friends the Flahertys are giving a pool party."

"Yeah, I heard about it. I was even invited."

"You ought to come down and surprise Georgette."

"I don't think she wants any surprises right now."

"Women always love surprises. Take it from an old married man."

"Not this time. She even dropped the D word when I left down there. She's angry that I didn't stay for the interview with the detectives."

"Uh-oh. That's not good. So why didn't you stay?" He quickly added, "Sorry. None of my business."

"I had to get back. There's a lot going on up here. I knew she was in good hands with Jay."

"Oh, definitely. Jay's the best. So what are you going to do? Let her stay down here long as she wants?"

"Everybody gets to do what they want in my world."

"I hear you, but maybe if you showed up out of nowhere at that pool party, she'd get over her mad quicker."

"I'll think about it."

"Call me if you change your mind. I'll tell you how to get there. Better yet, I'll pick you up at the airport and take you there myself."

"If I go, I'll drive it. I'm beginning to know the Panhandle by heart. I could drive it with my eyes closed."

"Let me know. I'll back you up whatever you decide."

"Thanks, CJ. Don't think I will make it down there again, but let me know if you hear anything more about Eric."

"Will do. Later." He clicked off and I went out on the porch to think about this latest development, wondering if the homeless man Eric had killed was the same one the teenage jokester had abducted from his father's funeral home and driven around town showing off to his buddies.

Georgette came from a weird town all right. But then what's new? I was born and raised in Louisiana. We have our own strange people and our own skeletons up here, and plenty of them. The food's better in Louisiana though. Much, much better. Call me spoiled if you want, but a steady diet of bland seafood platters, French fries and soggy cole slaw in little paper cups just doesn't do it for me. And if a Florida restaurant has anything that says *Cajun* on the menu, run like hell for the parking lot and don't look back.

\* \* \*

Stubs drove up and got down a couple of hours later. We walked to the back and I showed him the work I'd done on the tool shed, then we threw a few balls for Hoss. Some rain the night before had cooled things off, but had brought out the mosquitoes, so we slapped at them until we had enough, then went into the house.

I told him a little about the pitchfork murder, leaving out most of the personal details, but said enough to let him know I was having a hard time making up my mind what to do next.

"Look, bro. You'd never catch me getting married so I'd never be in this situation, but if I was....my wife wouldn't be roaming around four states away."

"Three states."

"Whatever. It wouldn't be happening. You better go down there and get her is the way I see it. Either that or cut her loose."

"Like I said, I think she needs some time out."

"Time out, my ass. You're either married or you aren't. Go down there and get her at that party and bring her home, or else leave her down there. Adios."

"*Un coeur noir,*" I said, smiling at him.

"That's me," he laughed. "And that's why I'm not married. You hear anything more about Ho-Ho?"

"They picked him up but not so he would know they scoped out Gervis' camp. They had to let him go. He's a good bullshitter. However, the Chief is sure he'll run his mouth one day before too long and then they'll have him by the short hairs."

"The Chief is right. Get a few shots of white whiskey down Ho-Ho, and he will be bragging on what a notorious outlaw he is."

"How long before you figure they set up shop again for the rooster fights?"

"I'm guessing they're ready about now."

"Sheriff Quebedeaux is ready for opening night. This will be good."

"Maybe you and I should ride out there tonight and see if anything's going on. Should be a good show to watch them get busted."

"Can't do it."

"Why not?"

"Cause I think you've talked me into driving back down to Florida. Would you mind keeping an eye on the place and watching Hoss again?"

Stubs clapped me on the back. "Sure thing, bro. Go bring back your woman or leave her down there. One or the other. That's just the way it is."

# 40

# THE POOL PARTY

And that is how I ended up walking into the Flahertys' elegant frame house on Bonita City Bay with C.J. that Saturday ready to surprise Georgette. The night before I had checked into a motel miles from The Cottages and she had no idea I had driven down once again to the Gulf Coast.

We passed through a sprawling living room with three skylights and more couches than I'd ever seen in one house. The thermostat was set so low, you could have hung meat in there, and then we passed through sliding glass doors to a huge caged patio area with giant ceramic pots filled with palms and baby citrus trees and hanging plants that you had to bob and weave to avoid.

Beyond that was a fifty-foot rectangular pool with chaises and cushioned outdoor chairs all around it. At one end of the pool, there was a rattan bar shaded by an awning, an Hawaiian shirted bartender and a crowd of people milling around, waiting for their drinks. A live reggae band played under some palm trees on the far side of the pool halfway between the distant dock and the pool area. About fifty people were standing in groups of three and four talking, drinking, laughing, swaying to the music, while another dozen treaded water in the pool or swam laps or tossed a beach ball back and forth. A few people floated on inflated rafts kicking back with a drink in their hand.

Some of the guests had come by boat and there were a few ski boats tied up at the long dock and a Donzi muscle boat as well. Beyond the dock, a thirty-foot sloop was anchored in the Bay so at least one person had swum in for the party. The bartender must have been pouring strong drinks because the volume was cranked way up on the laughter and the conversations.

"You look around for Georgette while I get us a drink," C.J. said. "What you want?"

I pointed to a woman in a zebra striped bikini sipping a frosted Margarita with salt crusted rim. "I'll have what she's having."

"You're on. Be right back."

I spotted Georgette then. She was on the far end of the pool talking to a man wearing dark glasses and a canvas cap with the brim turned down. I walked toward them slowly, watching my step as people splashed water all over the lip of the pool.

As I came closer, I saw the man pick up her hand and hold it between his own. Puzzled, I stepped right up near them, but they were so engrossed they weren't aware of my approach.

"I have never forgotten you," he said with the exaggerated motions and slow speech of someone who has had too much to drink. "And you still look fantastic. It's remarkable. You haven't changed at all after all these years. You still look the same. I don't know why you avoided me at the reunion, but am so glad you came here today so I could see you again." By then I was close enough to see the man was Cy Morris.

He lifted the hand that covered hers and leaned over to kiss the back of it, then instead, he raised her hand and gazed at it. "And look, you're even still wearing that same dazzling emerald ring from all those years ago. Déjà vu."

He lowered his head to kiss her hand, and just then she yanked back her arm, and as he looked up in surprise, she punched him, giving it all she had right at his nose.

There was a loud crack as she connected in just the right spot and he flew backwards, splashing down into the deep end of the pool as a woman treading water nearby screamed and backpedaled out of his way. Water splashed all over both of us, and for the first time Georgette saw me.

"Edmond. Edmond." She pointed to Cy who was still underwater. "He's the one. The pig was watching us that night," she hissed for only my ears. "He's the one who butchered Myron."

C.J. came up then holding the margaritas. "What the hell?" He handed the drinks off to a man stepping up to the scene. "Hold these for me, Burt?"

We both leaned over the edge of the pool to see Cy dropping like a stone to the bottom.

Georgette shaded her eyes with her hand as she stared at where Cy had gone down.

I jumped in and dragged Cy by the arms to the surface and then hooked my arm under his chin and held his face above water as he started sputtering, his nose bleeding all over my shirt. I hauled him to the edge of the pool and C.J. helped me pull him out.

"Man, talk about landing a sucker punch," C.J. said, talking over the loud reggae that was still playing. Mallory hurried up to him then and kneeled down beside him asking, "What happened?"

Cy blinked, still dazed. He shook his head, then started to rise, but with a woozy look around, lay back down again. A crowd of guests gathered around us. The hostess brought over a beach towel and wrapped it around his shoulders. His nose kept bleeding running in rivulets down onto the towel.

Cy's wife knelt beside him. "What did you do to her so she'd knock you out? Grope her?"

Cy mumbled, "Nothing. Kissed her hand. That's all I did. I swear."

"Kissed her hand?" The wife scowled up at Georgette from where she kneeled beside Cy. "What the hell is wrong with you, lady?"

"You'll find out soon enough," Georgette said to her. "Come on, Edmond, let's get out of here before I crack his skull open on the cement."

Georgette marched through the house and out the front door. "You have Detective Olson's number on your phone? I need to call him right away."

"I have it."

"Please dial it for me." She was still breathing hard and her face was red with anger. "Son of a bitch shoved a pitchfork through Myron. I'm going to see to it he's locked up for life or worse."

We stood at the end of the path leading to the street where my car was parked when Detective Olson answered the call. I handed the phone to Georgette.

"Detective Olson. This is Georgette Mallet. The man you want for Myron's murder is currently lying on his back poolside at the following address: 267 Oleander Drive. This is the Flaherty residence, and there is a birthday party going on that I just disturbed by punching Cy Morris in the nose and knocking him into the pool. How do I know it's him? Because he recognized a ring he would have no other way of knowing about, if he hadn't been watching and waiting that night in the barn when Myron gave it to me his last night on earth. I never wore that ring after that night because I was afraid someone might know Myron gave it to me. I never wore it again until I moved out of state. He's your man. You better get a warrant and get that Nova out of his garage while you still can before he figures out I'm on to him and hides it. With all the blood at that gory murder scene, there are bound to still be traces in the Nova."

She narrowed her eyes and took a deep breath. "I am not *trying* to tell you how to go about this. I *am* telling you how to go about this." She looked at me shaking her head. "Of course I know the ring I.D. isn't enough evidence, but I'm telling you Cy is your man. *Go get that Nova before he hides it, I'm telling you.* The Nova is all the proof you'll ever have."

"Yes, all right if we must. Give us about twenty minutes." She clicked off and narrowed her eyes at me. "He's doing the condescending thing on me, you know how I hate that. But let's go meet Detective Olson, shall we?"

"Wow, you are something else. Never knew you had it in you."

"He really aggravated me."

"Yeah, you stood up to Detective Olson, but I meant the sucker punch. You surprised the hell out of me with that one."

"You always told me if I ever had to punch somebody to give it all I got and go for the nose," she said, taking my arm. "Come on. Let's get this over with. The sooner the better."

# 41

# SHERIFF'S OFFICE

Detective Olson met with each of us separately. When we had both reported the poolside event and gone over every detail over and over as he taped our reports, he wrote it all up and had us sign as witnesses.

"How about giving me the ring now, please. I'll be right back. I have to take a picture of it for the file." Georgette slid the ring off her finger, handed it to him, and he left us alone for a few minutes.

I gave her an encouraging look. "You did fine," I said.

"Thanks. I'll be glad when we can get out of here though."

When Olson returned, he handed the ring back to her, sat back down at his desk and met her eyes. "If this goes to trial, we will require you to fly down here so you can testify for the prosecution. Is that understood? If it requires more than one day, we will put you up in a motel."

Georgette nodded with a glum look.

"That's it then. You both can leave," he said as though we'd been talking about the weather.

"Are you going to go get that Nova now?" Georgette asked.

"I don't discuss what we're going to do outside of the department. I'll be in touch." Dismissed with a slight lift of his hand, we left his office and filed out of the Sheriff's Office onto the sparse traffic of the late Saturday afternoon street.

"Friendly as hell, ain't he?" Georgette grumbled.

"He's not your friend," I said. "But he's on your side. He could have locked you up from the git go."

"Don't I know it," she said, shivering a bit and rubbing her arms at the very thought of it as we paused on the sidewalk and stared up at the four-story concrete County jail. Slits for windows gave it the look of a medieval fortress.

"Let's get back to The Cottages. I could use a drink," she said.

"We'll stop and pick up a bottle of wine. How's that?"

"Whatever. Just as long as it's wet and it's booze," she said. "I've had enough for one day."

# 42

# WRAP UP

After we'd had a glass of wine or two and Georgette had taken a shower and changed, we found a seafood restaurant on the Gulf and sat out on the deck so we could watch the sunset.

It was spectacular with peach, purple and vivid orange streaks and I took Georgette's hand as we sat, sipped our Margaritas and enjoyed the view.

"The Yankees might have ruined my hometown with all their ugly cement condos, but they haven't messed up the sunsets yet," she said. "You know," she leaned over and kissed my cheek, "I haven't had a migraine since you talked me into coming down here to tell my story."

"That's great."

"You know I never would have done it if you hadn't talked me into it."

I nodded.

"I dreamed about Myron last night. He didn't say anything, just looked at me from behind a gate. I had the strong feeling he was thanking me."

"I can believe it. He's glad you finally got around to it…for both your sakes."

"Thanks to you." She lowered her voice. "I'm sorry I was so mean to you. I don't want a divorce."

"Didn't think so. That's why I left you alone."

"Can we drive back tomorrow? I've been missing Hoss too."

"First thing when we wake up."

"And Buster?"

"Buster?"

"The tomcat at The Cottages."

"Oh, yeah. Him."

"The owner gave me a cat carrier somebody left behind."

"Oh, so you were already planning to come back before I came down to get you?"

"Nope. No matter how much I missed you, I wasn't going to budge until you came back down here to get me."

"Then how come you were getting ready to bring Buster back?"

"Cause I knew you would come back for me."

I set my drink down and then I set her drink down and I stood and pulled her to her feet and then we walked over to the railing of the deck and I held her in my arms and kissed her with that fabulous sunset in the background.

# 43

# THE BUST

As often happens with couples after a temporary breakup, we got along great after that. Once home in St. Beatrice, we were extra good to each other, grateful to be together and not on the path to divorce after all. Hoss even tolerated Buster, the new addition to the household. After all we'd been through, everything was peace and quiet at our house, and it felt great.

I was whitewashing a front porch column one afternoon when Stubs drove up in his GMC, radio blaring *I Can't Drive Sixty-Five.*

He cut across the grass from the driveway and stopped midway to talk to me.

"I heard rumors they're starting up tonight."

"Who? What?"

"The new rooster fight arena at Gervis' camp."

"Dumb. They haven't even gone to court yet for the old charges."

"They're so sure they'll get away with it. The word is out to meet at The Roadhouse parking lot where they'll all be picked up by an old school bus to take them to the new location. People who want to go won't know where the new pit is until they get there."

"Sounds about right."

"I'm going to listen in on the scanner this afternoon. If I hear of them getting ready for a bust, I'll call you to get ready. We can go watch."

"I don't know about that. The Chief told me to lay low, remember?"

"So? We'll wear black and lay low. It'll be fun. Like watching a movie."

"I'll think about it."

"You know you want to watch it all go down. I'll call you later. I'm getting out of here before you hand me a paintbrush." He headed back to the truck and I watched him back out, kicking up some gravel on the way. I had a feeling something would break that night, and I knew I'd want to go watch, just like Stubs had predicted.

* * *

Stubs got it right again. That was the night for the second bust, and we were waiting and watching for it. We had parked off the road and away from the parked patrol cars pulled off into a dirt lane a hundred feet from the barbed wire fence of the camp.

Stubs wore a black tee shirt and a black leather vest. I was wearing dark clothes also, so we could approach close enough to see what was going on without being seen. We walked up as far as the barbed wire, barely able to see the lights of the camp and the silhouette of the school bus parked near to the metal building.

"Let's get closer," Stubs said.

"Let's not," I said. "We don't want to be mistaken for part of the crowd."

"That building is small. Remember the old days? Hundreds of people came out for the fights."

"Yep. They sure did."

We didn't have long to wait before the show began. Suddenly out of the black trees surrounding the metal building, deputies started running toward the doors and windows, front and back. There was shouting and yelling and cursing as they stormed the building and then entered.

It didn't take five minutes before all was quiet.

"That was quick," said Stubs.

"The people in there are smart enough to not argue with men with guns."

After a few more minutes, some of the patrol car engines started up from back in the lane, and headlights came on as they drove slowly out of the woods and down the road to the front gate of the camp.

"They're going in to load up the prisoners."

"Load em up. Drive em out. Rawhiiide," Stubs sang.

The cruisers drove inside the camp toward the building, then turned around to face out, waiting in line as other deputies led out cuffed men, and with hands on the crown of each head, placed them into the back seat of the patrol cars, two to a car. Then they started loading up the school bus with the rest of the participants. We waited in the shadows as the cars edged back out to the road and turned left to go back to Eustis and the Parish jail.

"See, now aren't you glad I talked you into coming out for this?" Stubs asked, slapping at a mosquito. "That was more fun than a *Smokey and the Bandit* movie."

"Well, nothing's that much fun," I said, laughing.

"Pretty near," he said, and we turned around to go back to his truck.

"And by the way, The Bandit never got caught."

"True."

As we walked by the side of the road, one of the last of the cruisers passed us, and the interior light suddenly clicked on. Ho-Ho was sitting by the rear window and he peered out at us as the car passed, nodding his head and then making a spitting gesture against the glass.

"Uh-oh. Did Ho-Ho see us?" Stubs asked.

"What was your first clue? He was spitting at us."

"Bet now he thinks we're the ones who scoped his new location out."

"Looks like it."

"You know what he did to the last snitch," Stubs said.

I laughed. "Yeah, but we can both swim. So no worries."

# AFTERWORD

S hortly after we returned home to St. Beatrice, C.J. called to tell us of the headlines in the *Bonita City Observer*. "It's on all over in every TV news show. The paper is full of it. Can you read it online? Do you want us to send you the clippings?"

The headline read: NOTORIOUS PITCHFORK MURDER SOLVED? A photo of Cy beneath it showed him being escorted into the County Courthouse, sandwiched between Detective Olson and another detective. Cy's nose was swollen and bruised, but he stood ramrod straight and held his head tilted back as he stared straight ahead, his mouth tight, his expression defiant.

The article went on to say the Crime Unit had gone over the Nova with ultraviolet and picked up old bloodstains. Those stains were a match for the blood-drenched clothing Myron wore the night he was murdered. Clothing that was saved in a cardboard evidence box. Cy denied any involvement and stated he had no idea how the bloodstains could be in his car.

It went on to say that Cy's bail bid was denied owing to the infamy of the case and the judge's fears of flight risk.

"Do you want to subscribe to the paper so we can follow this?" I asked Georgette.

"Maybe just the online subscription. Don't think I want all those newspaper articles coming into our home every day. This will be going on for weeks. It will be a constant reminder and I want to put it all behind me. Online we can just check in on it if we want to."

Cy stayed in jail for six months before his trial. When the trial began, Georgette had to fly down there and testify as to what she knew. She stayed one night with Mallory and C.J. and they went with her to court. When she flew back, I picked her up in Lafayette and brought her home.

Cy was found guilty and sentenced to life in prison. Myron's parents were both dead, but his sister was interviewed after the trial and said it wouldn't bring Myron back, but she was satisfied with the verdict. "It took a long time. He was lucky he got to live free for twenty years. My brother never got to live his life."

As far as the administrative leave, it all went as we believed it would. The investigation wrapped up stating I was within my rights to shoot a man who had just shot at me. Internal Affairs found that I had not used my weapon in any way that went against prescribed departmental protocol. The Chief cleared me to return to full duty two weeks after we returned home.

The Crime Lab found Gus's DNA to be a match for the DNA in the spittoon. The Chief sent Dwight to arrest Gus for the burglary and the car theft because he thought sending me would "rub too much salt in the wound." I heard through the grapevine that Gus swore he'd get even with me one day, no matter how long it took. It looks like it will take a while, because he's in Angola now on a six-year sentence, so even if he just does one for two, I have a while before I have to start watching my back again.

Because they had opened up for business just weeks after the first bust, the judge was angry and gave the Duchamps, Sr. and Jr., and the other organizers three years jail time, two years suspended. Since they had not yet been to trial and convicted on the first felony, they were sentenced as if it were just one felony. All the other fifty people rounded up at the rooster fights were named as participants, but their sentences were all suspended.

Ho-Ho was so anxious to prove how dangerous and how bad he was to his cellmate that he told him what had happened to his last snitch, Skinny Dupuis. How he fought him on the bayou bank, and when Skinny fell over into the water, how he abandoned him to figure out how to either swim or drown.

He didn't realize who his cellmate was. In Louisiana it's wise to be cautious about bloodlines, and I'm not just talking about thoroughbreds. Skinny had cousins scattered all over four parishes, and Ho-Ho was mouthing off to a third cousin from

Coteau Holmes, a tiny, isolated swamper community where I felt quite sure Ho-Ho thought no one
had ever heard of Skinny Dupuis. I'm betting on a
Negligent Homicide verdict coming in soon as this
goes to trial.

Since Georgette is now headache free, she is
back at work. Only now she is not working in a travel
agency; she has decided she likes Forensics and is
working in the Sheriff's Office as a dispatcher and
studying Forensics online at night.

All in all, it was probably the most interesting administrative leave any cop ever had. Two cold-case
homicides were solved in Florida because I had the
time to stir things up, and I managed to solve our
burglary and car theft at home as well. And yes, Gus
has to pay restitution to Walter Crosby in Rye, Texas
for the two thousand Walter had paid for the stolen
Mustang, but that will take a while since Gus is un-
employed while vacationing in Angola.

I can't take credit for solving Skinny's drowning,
but I helped put the focus on Ho-Ho because of my
tip about the deer cameras. Stubs gets the credit for
locating Ho-Ho and the new rooster fight arena, but
I helped Stubs, and I still have the nasty white scars
from Satan's teeth to prove it.

Made in the USA
San Bernardino, CA
25 August 2014